He Set Her From Him,

and she missed the sweet wine taste of his mouth. "I won't lie, Mary. I want to take you to bed. Badly."

Her laughter was soft, her smile dismissive. "Find someone else. I'll only be here a matter of months, and I don't intend to have a casual fling."

"It won't be a casual fling, I promise you. For the moment I'll abide by your rules, but I warn you that I intend to change your mind, Dr. Mary Margulies."

Dear Reader:

There is an electricity between two people in love that makes everything they do magic, larger than life. This is what we bring you in SILHOUETTE INTIMATE MOMENTS.

SILHOUETTE INTIMATE MOMENTS are longer, more sensuous romance novels filled with adventure, suspense, glamor or melodrama. These books have an element no one else has tapped: excitement.

We are proud to present the very best romance has to offer from the very best romance writers. In the coming months look for some of your favorite authors such as Elizabeth Lowell, Nora Roberts, Erin St. Claire and Brooke Hastings.

SILHOUETTE INTIMATE MOMENTS are for the woman who wants more than she has ever had before. These books are for you.

Karen Solem
Editor-in-Chief
Silhouette Books

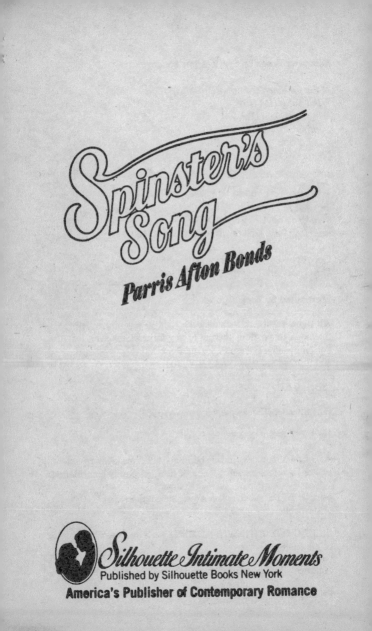

Spinster's Song

Parris Afton Bonds

Silhouette Intimate Moments
Published by Silhouette Books New York
America's Publisher of Contemporary Romance

Silhouette Books by Parris Afton Bonds

Made for Each Other (ROM #70)
Wind Song (IM #5)
Widow Woman (IM #41)
Spinster's Song (IM #77)

SILHOUETTE BOOKS,
300 E. 42nd St., New York, N.Y. 10017

Copyright © 1984 by Parris Afton Bonds
Cover artwork copyright © 1984 George Jones

Distributed by Pocket Books

ISBN: 0-671-47132-5

First Silhouette Books printing January, 1985

10 9 8 7 6 5 4 3 2 1

America's Publisher of Contemporary Romance

Printed in the U.S.A.

For Suzanne,
a Flare Child

Once upon a time there were a Spinster and a
Bachelor . . .

Chapter 1

THE TWO MEN STOOD BENEATH THE CANVAS AWNING OF the mustard-colored *tienda,* a small family-owned grocery store. They watched the Mustang, pulling a rented moving trailer, wheel down Kingdom Come's main street. Though it was not yet ten in the morning, a shimmering June heat distorted the windowpanes of the randomly spaced shops and businesses. A stout farm wife in jeans and flip-flops window-shopped desultorily, and the new head of the Border Patrol for that sector parked his pale green four-wheel-drive vehicle before the corrugated tin U.S. duty station.

The shorter of the two men, a swarthy replica of the flour commercial's doughboy, said, "The doctor—*es una soltera,* Rafe."

Rafe—tall, bronzed, with the fierce uncompromis-

ing features of his Castilian conquistador heritage—
said nothing. His eyes were of an unusual brown
matrix, flinted with gold. Above the butter-colored
handlebar mustache they were slitted against the
intense glare of the West Texas sun, still red and low
on the horizon.

The same superstitions to overcome, Rafe thought
dismally. Time had not changed his people—and
progress had not touched them.

That the doctor was a woman affected his people
less than the fact she was unmarried. A spinster. *Una
soltera.* The female doctor would find it difficult
establishing a practice in Kingdom Come. Not the
promising future the Ministry Outreach Services had
hoped for for the isolated farming and ranching
community.

He contained his exasperation. The years spent
with the Special Forces had not improved his patience. "I will see to the doctor, Vicente."

The round little man grinned. "I thought you
would, Rafe. You are not one to let pass a *bonita
mujer,* eh, *compadre?*"

So the doctor was not only a spinster but a pretty
woman. With but a rising flicker of interest, Rafe
pushed back his sweat-stained Stetson. He considered
himself a decent sort who sincerely liked women. No,
loved them. And that was his problem. Too much
loving with Barbara Sue the night before. She was a
wild tigress who didn't demand any permanency in a
relationship.

*   *   *

"Damn!"

Mary Margulies remembered she had latched the screen door. Indecisively she looked down at the inviting tub full of water. Cold water, since the water heater didn't work. But a cool, invigorating bath was just what her sweaty, aching body needed after unloading four big moving boxes.

Yet the milkman was supposed to leave two quarts of milk in her refrigerator that afternoon. And under the furnace blast of the high desert's skies the milk would quickly sour if left on the porch. Reluctantly she forsook the immediate pleasure of the bath to pad, naked but for a towel, along the stuccoed hallway. Beneath her bare feet the hard, unglazed mud tiles were refreshingly cool.

Empty cardboard boxes were strewn all the way into the tiny but serviceable rustic kitchen. An obsolete water pump still flanked the chipped porcelain sink's chrome faucet. The kitchen was crowded with unpacked boxes of pots and pans and dinnerware that mounded almost to the heavy wooden beams, called *vigas*, in the ceiling. She wove her way through the maze of boxes to the screen door and unlatched the hook.

Outside, the sun's white-hot brightness hurt the eyes, and the locusts hummed their perennial summer song. A dust devil spun down the empty caliche road, hopped one of the many canals that irrigated the valley and danced off across the cotton fields to lose itself in the purple haze of the Sierra del Hueso Mountains on the Mexican side of the Rio Grande. Nothing had altered in that changeless land.

Six long, lonely months in that desolate, dusty wilderness. Could she do it? She had to. The National Health Service Corps didn't take lightly to someone reneging on a government debt, the repayment of which called for a two-year tour of duty—usually in a doctor-deprived area like the Appalachians' poverty-stricken coal-mining communities. Fortunately her fellowship in maternal and neonatal nutrition had earned her an exciting position in the Walter Reed Military Hospital doing research for the first year and a half.

But the twelfth hour had arrived for Cinderella. She was to serve her last six months of duty in Texas' border region. Hot. Vast. Arid. Empty. Only the Big Bend country was hotter, emptier. But for the rimming mountains and the sluggish, brown, life-giving river, the land was much like the New Mexico oil fields of her childhood years. Not something of which she wanted to be reminded.

Of course, her assignment could have been worse. She could have been posted to a prison dispensary or an Appalachian black-lung clinic, where hope was bleak. At least in Kingdom Come there would be the miracle of birth that still never failed to awe her.

Kingdom Come looked as if it had been abandoned between two craggy mountain ranges. It was located in an isolated narrow garden valley created by the Rio

Grande, where only five thousand people lived in the six-thousand-square-mile county.

The people of Kingdom Come, mostly Hispanics, shyly avoided her gaze. Since arriving in Kingdom Come that morning she had talked only with the paunchy Hispanic who was both the town's postmaster and owner of the *tienda,* from which the mail was distributed. He had directed her to the ancient Rancho Encantado and its abandoned *caporal*'s, or foreman's, quarters that she would be renting. Then, as a kindly afterthought, Vicente had added that he would send the milkman out to the adobe quarters later that afternoon.

She had driven across Rancho Encantado's stone bridge, which arched across a swift-flowing canal, and down the caliche road to park her Mustang beneath one of the ancient lime trees that abutted the small flat-roofed adobe quarters. For a long, disappointing moment she had stood in the heat that lay over the dull sagebrush and white stretch of desert beyond, just looking at the baked adobe with its hot pink walls and garish turquoise trim.

Farther down the caliche road was the main house, a *hacienda* patinaed a soft antique rose-brown by time and weather. It was large, imposing and anachronistic. She had expected the *hacienda*'s owner or maybe someone from the Catholic Mission's Ministry Outreach Services to be there to meet her.

The Santo Tomás Mission, one of the oldest in the United States, had applied to the NHSC for a physician for the rural community of Kingdom Come. The

Mission's Ministry Outreach Services had agreed both to locate a house which she could rent and to renovate the derelict tannery shop in which she could set up her practice during that final six-month stint.

Shrewdly, the NHSC counted on a physician liking the assigned area and its people enough to continue the practice permanently.

Not her. She had already submitted her application to the prestigious Scott-Waggoner Medical Complex outside Washington, D.C. A letter from the Complex's recruiting director had informed her that she was one of the physicians under final consideration—upon successful completion of her obligation to NHSC, of course. The salary was this side of heaven for a doctor just out of medical school—and enough so she could finish educating the younger brother and sister who for so long had depended on her.

Was Amy dating yet? At eighteen she was certainly old enough. But then, Amy had absorbed a lot of her older sister's psychological makeup. The drive to escape the environs of poverty and ignorance and disease overrode any temporary infatuation. No, Amy had college to complete, and she wasn't likely to become seriously enamored of a young man until the shackles of the past were buried.

And Billy—why didn't he write more often? Though he was a year older than Amy, he didn't seem as certain about what he wanted from life. What if he got mixed up in drugs like Sam, the oldest of the boys, had? All her scolding and begging had not prevented her brother's fatal overdose. And there was Michael, who was in prison for homicide and, oh God, the others . . . the brothers and sisters who had died early in life from improper nourishment, or been relegated to foster homes.

There had been nine of them. A fatherless family who had needed guidance. By the time she was sixteen—and her mother dead—she was trying to keep the family unit together. And now that she was gone . . .

Just as she turned from the screen door, the sound of a vehicle rolling into the adobe's driveway reached her, followed by the slamming of a car door.

The milkman.

The obstacle course of boxes loomed ahead of her. She dashed for the nearest concealment, the closet housing the water heater. Huddling breathlessly in the dark, cramped closet, she felt utterly foolish. How many people, she silently inquired of the enameled water heater beside her, would trust their health to a doctor who hid almost birthday-naked in a closet?

The screen door's hinges squeaked, and a man's voice, deep and resonant, with the slightest accent, called out, "Dr. Margulies?"

She bit her bottom lip until it hurt. Looking down into the black abyss where her bare feet must be, she fervently prayed, *Just put the milk in the refrigerator and go away. Please.*

A long, agonizing moment later, sunlight flooded the closet. Horrified, her hazel-gray eyes looked up—and up—past a blur of scuffed boots and low-slung jeans, past a denim workshirt open to the waist . . . and into a very startled and very masculine face.

Premature rigor mortis, triggered by the most abject embarrassment, set into her body. At that moment an errant russet curl chose to tumble from the mass of hair skewered atop her head. It fell across her short nose that was bridged with the remnants of childhood freckles. Life flowed back into her, and she pursed her lips and blew on the bothersome tendril.

Above a *bandido* mustache the man's eyes, golden brown like the West Texas sand, stared at her with a look of bemusement. Indeed, they both stared at one another in shocked silence, their mouths unable to form words.

At last, pushing back his battered brown Stetson, he said, "Well, hel-lo."

Now those eyes glittered with barely controlled amusement and lusty male appreciation. His gaze flicked down the length of her small and almost nude body. The hair on her nape prickled. His tall frame, roped with sinewy muscle, seemed to fill the confining closet dangerously.

Her lips refused to cooperate. "What . . . what are you doing here?"

"I've come to fix the water heater."

"I was expecting the milkman."

She was certain a smile twitched the corners of his drooping mustache.

"Of course," he said with elaborate politeness. "I'll come back another time." With that he closed the door on her—quietly, firmly.

Seconds later she heard the screen door slam shut and a car drive away. Sweat beaded her upper lip and rolled down her slanted cheekbones. Her knees were as shaky as those of a rickets victim. Her old friend, heartburn, ulcerated through her stomach, and at that moment she could have swallowed a whole packet of antacids.

"Damn!" How could such a thing happen to a woman who valued her dignity at all costs?

"Damn!"

Chapter 2

FATHER JOHN, LOOKING AS SPRIGHTLY AS A LITTLE OLD elf, stood before the glistening white mission's high grillwork doors and pointed out the direction of the renovated tannery—the future facility for Mary's clinic.

The sun was burning the top of her head, where her center part stood. Her hair, unruly when unbound, could be described as dark fire, and beneath the sun's blistering glare her head felt as if it were indeed ablaze. After that year practicing in Washington, D.C., she had forgotten how in the desert the mere act of drawing a breath could sear all the way to the lungs. And it was just June, with the worst of the dry summer heat yet to come.

Wisely she had knotted her wildly curling hair up off her neck, but already damp corkscrew tendrils were spilling down its white length. To combat the heat she had chosen a lightweight lime-colored suit of seersucker with a mist-green blouse.

Surely Father John was hot in his priest's black garb and high, stiff clerical collar. But beneath the thatch of shaggy white hair his time-lined face beamed benignly.

Could word have circulated yet of the humiliating incident the day before? It certainly wasn't a very good impression to make on the citizens of Kingdom Come—a naked doctor found hiding in the closet with the water heater. At the mere thought she felt an embarrassing flush scorch her face, not for the first time in the past twenty-four hours.

"The desert climate takes some getting used to, my daughter," Father John said, mistaking her suddenly crimson complexion for a result of the heat. "By now Rafael Anaya has started up the tannery's evaporative cooler, and you can get out of this hot sun. I do wish I could be of more help, but it was Rafael's idea for the Church's Ministry Outreach Services to bring a doctor into Kingdom Come, and the church board and I have left all the details to him." The old man's faded blue eyes twinkled. "But I don't think anyone expected a woman doctor, least of all Rafael."

The tannery was located on one of the dusty back streets, certainly not a hygienic setting. But the pink-blossomed mimosas and graceful willows that surrounded the white cinder-block building provided a screen for the occasional dust storms that whipped across the land. And the tannery's interior, bare of furniture but for an old reception desk, was immaculately clean.

No antiseptic smell pervaded the building, which pleased her, for she found that the overpowering, manufactured odor made patients uneasy. Instead the reception room was redolent of the aroma of soft leather and the faintly lingering smell of the lime solution used to tan the leather.

From the rear of the tannery she could hear hammering, and she wandered through another door into an immense room that must once have been the workshop. The man's back was to her as he drove another nail into the plasterboard that would partition the large room into two smaller ones.

He wore no shirt, and sweat streamed down the ravines created by the flexing of his muscles. The skin that sheathed his wide shoulders was beautifully bronzed—whether by the sun or heritage, it was difficult to tell. The churned-butter-colored hair, as curly as her own, writhed down to his nape.

"Mr. Anaya?" she called, but the noise of the hammering overrode her softly modulated voice.

She crossed to him, and as he stopped hammering to remove a nail clamped between his teeth, the heels of her white spectator pumps clicked briskly against the concrete floor, echoing loudly in the vast room. He looked over his shoulder, and she halted at the sight of gold-flecked eyes in a powerfully virile face.

"No!" she said in a strangled whisper. The man from yesterday. The man who had found her in the closet.

His contained expression in no way acknowledged that he recognized her, and for that she was grateful. His lips, mobile yet strongly set, smiled—a lethal, lung-stunning smile in keeping with the eyes' appreciative assessment of her. "You are Dr. Margulies." It was a statement, not a question.

Sudden realization, followed by disbelief, flooded her. "You're coordinating the NHSC program here?"

His fingers shoved back the sweat-dampened yellow-brown curls from his forehead, and a smile curled beneath the rakish handlebar mustache. "Father John would like to think so."

As if that explained all he deemed necessary, he laid the hammer in the open tool chest at his feet and reached for the sun-bleached blue shirt draped over the sawhorse behind him. Shrugging into his shirt, he said, "The NHSC neglected to inform us of your exact arrival date, so I have to apologize for the uncompleted state of your clinic."

She was still too stunned to assimilate anything of what he was saying, and merely nodded when he said, "Why don't we get a cup of coffee? I'll tell you a little about the town and its people while we wait for the water cooler to lower the temperature in here."

When he touched her elbow it was *her* temperature that suddenly needed to be lowered. Whether it was the fact that this man had seen her naked, or that his raw masculinity threatened to breach her carefully erected wall of detachment, she wasn't certain.

Incredible—getting giddy as a girl at her age. She wasn't about to lose her head and heart over a man just when her career was at last getting started. There burned in her brain the memory of her mother scraping by doing menial jobs in order to keep the family together until those last agonizing days before her untimely death, and the knowledge that she herself meant to make it easier for Billy and Amy. The other six—she no longer had to worry about them.

The Oasis Restaurant was a World War II-vintage Quonset hut rimmed with fan-leafed palms and tall spiked yucca. Though it wasn't yet lunchtime, cowboys and roughnecks and railroad men were already drifting into the Oasis' separate barroom. Rafe found the two of them an empty booth toward the rear of the oblong room with bark-thatched walls and hollowed coconut shells for candle holders. The lighting was dim enough that the blue checkered tablecloths didn't spoil the restaurant's attempt at a lush, islandy effect.

He placed their order with the plump teenage waitress, ordering hot tea for himself—which surprised Mary. With the disreputable-looking Stetson pulled low over his forehead and the fierce mustache, he looked more like the cold-beer cowboy type in the television commercials. After the waitress left, he withdrew a cigarette package from his shirt pocket and offered her one.

"No, thank you," she murmured. What she needed was a roll of antacids. Funny after all these years how her stomach was beginning to act up again. This man's presence was obviously a contributing factor. She tried to judge his age. At least thirty or more, if his eyes were any indication. In their golden depths glimmered vast experience, in which she strongly suspected that the female sex played a major part.

She unfolded the paper napkin in her lap. "Somehow I can't quite picture you working for a church."

The match flared and threw the rugged planes and hollows of his face into relief. "I don't." His grin would have been lecherous if it weren't for the little-boy charm that sparkled in the eyes. "But I *was* an altar boy for Father John."

"Why is it I find that piece of information difficult to put in perspective?"

"Perhaps I don't look the angelic type," he offered in a bantering tone.

She rejected his light approach. "But you *are* helping him. Why?"

The grin and the sparkle momentarily disappeared. "After Vietnam and a slew of other revolution-torn countries, I was sick of the things I had seen . . . and done. I wanted the peace and anonymity of the valley again. Father John's a con artist. He spotted an easy touch. He depends on me—more than he should."

The last was added with a travesty of a smile. But his flat unemotional tone when he talked of his prior life almost made her shiver. He had an ability to project menace and vulnerability at the same time. "If you don't work for the mission, then what do you do?"

"You might say I'm a cotton farmer." His lips curved in a smile that almost leveled her. "And I'm your landlord, Dr. Margulies."

"That's why you came to fix the water heater yesterday!"

Warm laughter lurked in his thick-lashed eyes. "Do you always dress like that for the milkman?"

Oh, for just one antacid tablet. She concentrated on spreading the paper napkin in her lap and said frostily, "That's a highly improper question."

His eyes fastened on her mouth in a way that told her that he wanted very much to kiss it. "But you were in a highly improper state."

Somehow she had to carry this off. "Please—don't remind me." She forced an aloofness into her gaze to counteract his twinkling expression and said in the firm but reasonable voice that she used on her patients, "I reacted like a child to a most embarrassing situation. I assure you that it won't happen again."

With a perfectly straight face he said, "Well, we certainly can't go on meeting like that, Dr. Margulies."

She was suddenly intensely aware that she was a woman, a knowledge that she had suppressed for so long that she had forgotten how it felt.

Dangerous. He was very dangerous.

The waitress brought their order, allowing Mary some time to regroup her defenses. "Tell me about Kingdom Come," she said, then busied herself emptying a packet of diet sweetener into her coffee cup. At thirty-five, maintaining a hundred and fifteen pounds on a five-foot-three-inch frame did not come easily.

The man opposite her took her cue and ground out

his cigarette. "You'll find the climate of Kingdom Come refreshing after you adjust." His hands engulfed the delicate cup as he drank his tea. She liked his hands. They weren't the soft hands of a businessman, but capable, powerful ones with long, supple fingers and blunt, callused tips.

"The summer nights are cool," he continued, "and the low humidity moderates the hot days. The winters are mild, and the sun has failed to shine only thirty-nine of the last 6,586 days."

She had to smile. His humor was irrepressible. "You also work for the Kingdom Come Chamber of Commerce?"

His strong white teeth flashed in a grin. "Kingdom Come is only an hour and a half away from El Paso and Juarez, and three hours from the ski slopes of Cloudcroft."

She leaned her oval chin on one fist. "Tell me more."

"You've got gorgeous eyes, Doctor. And adorable freckles."

She frowned. "I'm immune to flattery, Mr. Anaya."

He shrugged charmingly. "I tried."

"Kingdom Come?" she prompted.

He sighed and continued his tour-guide parody. "The community was originally part of a Spanish mission compound, but when the Rio Grande changed her course, the compound became a part of Texas. The forty-niners and gamblers and ladies of the night going to California, and later the Anglo farmers and cattlemen who arrived with the railroad, called the place Kingdom Come because—"

"Because it looked like the end of the world." She grinned.

His laughter came easily, pleasing her. "Exactly."

She picked up her own cup, and the hot coffee threw steam into her face. After swallowing a sip she said, "But you aren't telling me everything. What about the people?"

"Like I was saying—ranchers, farmers, some railroad men, a few roughnecks and roustabouts, and mostly migrant laborers."

"Then the clinic is going to be quite busy."

"No."

Carefully she replaced the cup in its saucer and met his level gaze. "Just what are you saying?"

He was all business now, the pursuit of the fairer sex momentarily shelved. "That you are going to come up against a wall of prejudice, Dr. Margulies. Kingdom Come is largely Hispanic. The people go to the local *curandera* for the treatment of their ills."

"*Curandera?*"

"A healer of sorts. Operates through faith and herbs. Of course, there are the Anglos. Mostly old-timers. But even the younger ones have families who settled this valley as far back as the end of the Civil War. You, Dr. Margulies, are an outsider—and a woman at that. 'Not a real doc,' they'll say. When they get sick and need a doctor, they prefer to drive up to El Paso."

"I don't believe someone would be so obstinate in an emergency."

His eyes mocked her. "You've been here scarcely more than twenty-four hours. Do you know what the people call you? *La soltera*. The spinster."

She controlled her surprise. One who spins—the age-old occupation of a single woman. An older woman. "I am a spinster by choice, Mr. Anaya."

His lips curled, raising the ends of his mustache. "I don't doubt that."

She didn't have to add that there had been plenty of opportunities to change that status. Modesty aside, she knew she was very attractive. But she didn't play on that asset. Rather she relied on her capabilities, her intelligence and the honest warmth she felt for the patients with whom she dealt to help her bridge difficulties.

In med school she had been pursued by the young male students and the older professors. Perhaps it was her lack of eagerness that made her appear overly selective, a quality her peers resented. She found it amusing that they labeled her a snob. Mary Margulies, from the wrong side of the tracks, a snob.

"I have been on my own since I was six. The summer I turned ten, I outfought a boy for the right to throw newspapers. I can assure you, Mr. Anaya, that I am quite capable of handling difficult situations."

His precisely delineated bottom lip seemed to quiver. "Now, just why is it, Dr. Margulies, that I feel like Kingdom Come didn't know what a difficult situation was—until you hit town?"

Chapter 3

LA JEAN DODSON STEPPED BACK FROM THE FRESHLY painted plasterboard and said, "A masterpiece, if I say so myself."

Mary put her hands on her hips and peered through her lashes at the last wall of the clinic to be painted. Easter-egg-blue paint splotched her jeans in several places and streaked one cheekbone. No pale green paint for her clinic. Despite what psychologists had said about the calming effects of the color, to her it was a bland, unhealthy shade.

She pushed back the swath of curls that dipped over one eye. "I think you're seeing something I'm not," she told her new receptionist with a grin.

The previous week Mary had placed an ad in the small weekly newspaper for a receptionist and had just about despaired of anyone answering it. Then in walked La Jean Dodson—a very tall divorcée with a very flat chest and very orange, very Afro hair. Mary would have hired La Jean for her gloriously kinky hair, if for no other reason. The thirty-five-year-old woman had chosen to move from El Paso to Kingdom Come three years earlier because she thought it would be a good place to raise her two children.

Mary was discovering that a small middle-class community did exist in the barren wastes of West Texas, a community replete with peewee soccer and baseball teams for the children and a comfortable suburb of modern, moderate-priced homes.

"When I saw your ad," La Jean had told Mary with a grin, "I immediately quit my job at the High Lonesome, waiting on tables. So you've got no choice but to hire me."

There was never any question that Mary would. She liked the perky woman. Then, too, she had waited on tables through high school and college and could sympathize with La Jean's desire to escape the menial drudgery.

Though the problem of a receptionist was solved with the hiring of La Jean, another problem reared its ugly head: how to pay a receptionist's wages, much less the installment note on the medical supplies and equipment she had ordered. And, of course, there had been the necessity of a car. The monthly payments on the Mustang had to be met, along with the rent and utilities and food and gas, the money she sent to Amy and Bill—and on and on.

Almost two weeks had passed since she had opened

her practice, and not a soul had wandered in. The prospect of maintaining a private practice in Kingdom Come for six months was bleak. Yet she had no choice. Fortunately the community and the Ministry Outreach Services subsidized the newly established clinic with a minimal—very minimal—contribution.

With a sigh she laid the paintbrush in the pan. "We now have an office, La Jean, but no patients. Do you have any suggestions?"

La Jean's cheerful grin hung in place. "We can import the bubonic plague. It's doing a good job in New Mexico at the moment."

Mary hefted the box of I.V.-solution bottles that had arrived by bus the day before and toted it toward the second examination room. "The people here would shrivel up and rot before they'd come to the clinic."

La Jean trailed her to the door and slouched her curveless frame against the doorjamb, crossing her arms. "No, most of them would go to old Josefita— the *curandera*. The others, the *ricos*—our more prosperous farmers and ranchers—they'd make the drive up to El Paso."

With a grunt Mary knelt to push the box onto the bottom shelf below the counter and closed the cabinet door. "Just what Mr. Anaya warned."

La Jean grinned and chewed enthusiastically on her gum. "So you've met Kingdom Come's most eligible bachelor. There's not a woman in the valley who's safe from him—or one that wants to be, for that matter. Damned good-looking stud, isn't he?"

Mary stood and dusted her hands. "I was so tired last week," she evaded, "that I wouldn't have noticed had he looked like Quasimodo."

"With that kind of charm, it wouldn't matter to the women here, including myself, if he had a hunched back!"

For all the truth her receptionist's statement held, Mary knew that La Jean was seeing a border patrolman by the name of Eddie Williams and was crazy about the man, who she declared had been let loose by the gods to run amok among womankind.

"If Rafe has a hump hidden somewhere," La Jean continued, "Christina Andersson sure isn't complaining." Working on her gum, she thought a moment, then added with a snort, "She might even go for something like that."

"Rafe or the hump?"

La Jean hooted with laughter. "Both. You know how the spoiled, bored types are."

Mary contained her laughter. "No, I don't know anything about spoiled, bored types, having never been around the *ricos* of the world."

And she didn't want to know about anyone who had anything to do with Rafe Anaya. That man was walking trouble for her equilibrium. She repressed her curiosity for a full thirty seconds. "Just who is Christina Andersson?"

La Jean grinned. "I thought you'd never ask. Her father is into megabucks. You know—the typical tycoon. Owns the newspaper, is board chairman of the Valley Bank, and is part-owner of several small pecan farms in the valley."

"And Christina?"

"Christina's barely twenty, but our Scandinavian beauty has been love-struck since she was thirteen and Rafe gave up some kind of military career and returned to Kingdom Come and Rancho Encantado."

A soldier—that explained the lethal aura that remained just below the easygoing surface. By this time she also knew that he was no mere cotton farmer. Rancho Encantado was the seat of three thousand acres. Yet several times that week, when she'd left for work early in the morning, she had spotted him hunkered down in the fields alongside the other laborers, his blondish-brown curls easily identifiable among the Mexican-Americans who had Indian blood mixed with their Hispanic heritage.

Why did he work like a common laborer when he was obviously a moving force in the community? He was dichotomous—a hard worker and a playboy. A golden-eyed blond and a Mexican-American. A past soldier and present farmer. And an arrogant, utterly charming rake.

Enough. Mary grabbed her black bag of examination instruments from the counter. "I'm going home to change. Then, if Muhammad can't come to the mountain, the mountain will go to Muhammad."

Startled, La Jean straightened her six-foot frame. "Just what does that mean?"

"It means I'm going to treat the people of this valley come hell or high water."

"Hell will come first."

At the door Mary said over her shoulder, "Catch the phone for me."

"Fat chance of it ringing!"

"Thanks for your faith!"

"Watch out for the Border Patrol," La Jean called after her.

The sun beat down on the back of his neck, and he ached like hell from stooping. The position reminded him of the small bamboo cage he had occupied in Dnem Nou for three weeks. He stood and rubbed the back of his neck, while the farmers and laborers waited for him to continue the lecture.

It was beyond him why he had ever agreed to the University of Texas' El Paso branch's suggestion that he teach cotton farming and weed control that summer for the Agricultural Extension Service. Maybe it was a start in alleviating some of the human misery he had seen in so many third-world nations.

He rather doubted it, but he always finished a job he started. So he hunkered down again among the rows of tufted cotton hulls and resumed talking about range reclamation and weed control, in Spanish, for the benefit of the largely Hispanic group.

Fifteen minutes later, when Eddie braked the Border Patrol's Jeep at the side of the road, Rafe gratefully called it a day and dismissed the men. He ambled over to the Jeep and, bracing his hands on the door frame, eyed his friend glumly.

Eddie was as tall as Rafe, but lanky, with straight brown hair and a perpetual gleam in his dark blue eyes. "You look like you could use a cold beer, ol' friend. Or maybe a hot woman. Or maybe both."

Rafe thought of Mary Margulies, who was anything but hot. She could maintain that cool composure at all times; it hadn't even cracked when he had caught her nearly buck naked. At that a chuckle erupted, and Eddie said, "Gee, Rafe, did I say something funny?"

"A private joke." Just thinking about her, and he felt a distinct rise of interest. "Meet you at the High Lonesome in half an hour."

"Can't." Eddie glowered. "The chief has me doing trail drag along the river this evening."

A spindly spiral of dust announced a passing car, a Mustang. Both men watched it flash by toward an unknown destination. "Your new boarder, the spinster doctor," Eddie drawled. "Hear tell she looks as cuddly as a little kitten—and is as cool as a polar bear."

It was spoken mainly as a question, for if anyone would know all there was to know about a female, it was Rafe. But his mouth flattened, and Eddie observed, in mild shock, "Why, she's been in town two weeks and you haven't laid a finger on that beautiful body, have you, ol' friend?"

"And no one will," Rafe brooded, "if she has

anything to say about it." And if he had anything to say about it. No one except himself, of course.

The *barrio* was a cluster of homes scattered along the old swamplands that banked the river bottom—land that, before the construction of Elephant Butte Dam up in New Mexico, had flooded yearly. Land that no one had wanted then. The houses were more like shanties, part adobe, part corrugated tin, even cardboard. *Jacales,* they were called. Raw-sewage-laced yards that were dirt-smooth. Here and there a toddler sat playing in the dirt, sometimes naked.

Mary shouldn't have been surprised at the primitive conditions. As a flare child in the oil fields, she had grown up without any home at all. Unless one counted the car, parked in the winter months for warmth beneath the oil flares that burned off gas. Those people who had no homes and sought the flares' intense heat for their only source of warmth in the winter—those were the oil patches' flare people. And she and her brothers and sisters and all the homeless urchins of the transient families were the flare children.

If the Welfare Department hadn't stepped in . . . But then she would never have been hospitalized for rheumatic fever. Never had the opportunity to make that fateful decision to become a doctor.

She halted the Mustang before a *jacal* that was almost obscured by the line of washed clothing stretched between two mesquites. As she walked toward the door piglets rooting at the sun-baked earth trotted off, squealing and grunting at the intruder.

The door's screen gapped in several places. She knocked on the frame, and a squat dark-skinned woman appeared but did not open the door.

"I'm Dr. Margulies."

The woman's flat face registered no welcome. Her gaze moved resentfully over Mary's tailored white linen suit. What next?

"I'm calling to see if I can help you with any health problem?"

No response.

Mary wasn't going to give up so easily. "May I come in, Mrs. . . . ?"

For a moment the woman eyed her stolidly. Then she pushed open the screen door and stepped back for Mary to enter. *"Soy* Señora Ofelia Ruiz," the woman mumbled.

A curtainless window provided the one room *jacal* with light. At Mary's entrance, a barefoot girl with cropped black hair moved to cower in a corner.

The air was stifling, and flies buzzed incessantly about, as if they were colonizing the house. Incredibly, the floor was dirt-packed. The woman folded her arms, as though saying, "Well?"

A mewling sound brought Mary's glance to the cardboard box sitting on a couch whose once-pink upholstery was punctured by springs. "Kittens?" she asked with a polite smile, determined to stay, if only for five minutes.

Ofelia Ruiz said nothing, and when Mary peeked

over the box's rim she was startled to see a baby. It was thin and undernourished. The little sunlight that shafted through the dust-filmed window showed eyes that were yellow. Jaundiced. It was more than just a "failure-to-thrive" baby. Most likely it had hepatitis.

Mary looked up at the mother. "May I examine your child?"

At last a flicker of emotion passed across the woman's face—a mother-hen sort of expression. She feared for her children. Superstition again.

"It's all right," Mary assured her. "I only want to help your child."

But the tongue blade that seemed to choke the baby, the magical penlight illuminating the tiny mouth's inflamed cavity, the gleaming otoscope appearing to poke dangerously at the ears—all these served only to upset the mother.

A stool culture was needed, and gamma-globulin injections if hepatitis was present. But the mother would obviously refuse to bring the child in to the clinic. "Your baby needs good foods. Baby foods. I'll bring some jars by. All right, Mrs. Ruiz?"

The woman's sharp chin barely dipped in acknowledgment. *"Sí, soltera."*

Not "doctor." That Spanish word for "spinster" again. Mary left, feeling useless. Her visits to other *jacales* revealed untreated burns, conjunctivitis, impetigo, sore throats. And more faces brooding with suspicion.

Driving back home, she considered the enormity of

the task that faced her. She knew that her only hope of reaching the people was through the *curandera,* old Josefita. And to go about that she would need Rafe Anaya's help. Only he seemed to be able to bridge both worlds. Only he seemed to be accepted by both modern civilization and its primitive counterpart.

By the time she wheeled the Mustang across the stone bridge, dusk was settling over the land, transforming the last light of day that lingered on the horizon into a frenetic display of fiery reds and pinks and oranges, and highlighting the spiked yuccas that were just beginning to blossom. There was a beauty in that barrenness, a Rembrandt-like richness of shadow.

Mary didn't bother to go inside and change, but set out down the gravelly drive to the rambling *hacienda.* The pebbles made walking in her heels difficult, and, regretting that she had not driven the short distance, she gave up and removed her shoes.

Rafe's maroon pickup was nowhere to be seen, although a white MG was parked before the tile-roofed carriage house that had been converted to a garage. Behind black wrought-iron grillwork the house's tall arched windows were dark. Discouraged at the thought of making the return journey down the gravelly drive, she leaned back against the courtyard's grillwork gate, listening to the splash of water in the stone fountain within. Maybe Rafe was right. Maybe a woman doctor had no—

The sound of tires grating on gravel broke her dismal train of thought. She opened her eyes and, still leaning against the gate, watched the pickup arrive, trailed by a tornado of dust. The pickup ground to a halt and Rafe swung out. His long legs were clad in white-dusted jeans, and he strode toward her with a feline grace that could never be construed as anything but totally masculine. In the half-light she could almost imagine him two hundred years earlier, stalking the *tierra incognita* in a conquistador's metal armor to conquer the savages for God, glory and gold—and, of course, conquer every female he could bundle into bed.

He braced a sun-bronzed hand above her head on the gate, and she was glad of the gate's support because—stupidly—she was shaken by the man's nearness. Odd, the power of chemical attraction. She reminded herself that it was only that—chemistry, convenience or circumstance—that caused two people to become involved in the first place. All the wrong reasons. Superficial reasons. She would not let herself fall into that trap.

"Is everything all right, Doctor?"

Regrettably, she liked his voice; it was low, with a husky Spanish accent. Its timbre sent pleasant tremors along her spine. "Why, yes. But . . . do you have a few minutes? I'd like to talk to you."

He leaned closer and said, "Gardenias! Your hair smells of gardenias."

"None of that, Mr. Anaya," she said sternly.

He eyed her innocently, but those pale brown irises seemed to dance. "Oh, well." He opened the gate. "Come on in."

Said the wolf to Little Red Riding Hood, Mary thought cynically. She hadn't realized how tall he was. In her stocking feet she barely reached his chest. Quickly she slipped her shoes on.

"You're even smaller than I judged, Doctor."

"That's because you have the advantage of boots," she pointed out in a matter-of-fact voice.

His hand touched the small of her back lightly, guiding her along the flagstone steps that were cracked here and there with age. "You can have your choice of cold beer or hot green tea."

She began to talk inanely to cover the catastrophic effect his mere touch had on her composure. "Somehow I don't picture you drinking green tea."

A glimpse of white teeth showed below the sweep of mustache. "After my first furry taste of the stuff, I didn't either. But thirst and custom can quickly convince you otherwise. Now I'm hopelessly addicted, Doctor."

The impersonal way he addressed her—"Doctor" —it was as if he were taunting her about her sexuality. Neuter. That's what one date had said of her. After that she didn't bother with dating. Getting her diploma was of primary importance anyway. She strove to keep a platonic relationship between herself and men. Yet in the deepening dusk this man's overwhelming masculinity made dispassion very difficult.

He opened one of the heavy hand-carved doors and switched on a wall light to reveal a large living room that looked more like that of a Mediterranean villa. The decor was a warm mixture of old and modern. A wall of glass looked out onto the faint stars ascending a pale pink sky. The terra-cotta-tiled floor was covered by a lush white wool carpet with a fringe border. The same earthen tile had been laid into the wall to surround the whitewashed fireplace. The room's stark, sparkling white was relieved by the heavy ceiling beams, the one long wall of books and the massive furniture.

A bachelor's den if there ever was one.

Hands on hips, he stood looking down at her. "Hardly austere, is it?"

Holy Moses, but he was beautiful. A golden beauty, with a devil-may-care look in those laughing eyes. The embodiment of a satyr, a fertility god. "The house certainly doesn't fit in with vows of poverty."

"Unfortunately I've been saddled with it since birth. The estate has been in the family for over two hundred years, and the guilt my grandmother unloads on me prevents me from dumping it." He grinned, adding, "And pleasure. Now, how about some tea?"

She followed him into the kitchen, which was almost as big as the living room. Like her adobe kitchen, the *hacienda*'s had been renovated with the most modern appliances. Yet it still retained a certain old-world charm.

A gleaming array of copper pans and brass utensils was suspended from a *viga,* catching the eye immediately. A used coffee cup sat in the stainless-steel sink, and envelopes and sections of the El Paso paper were strewn over the butcher-block table in the center of the kitchen. Mary sat in a cane-backed chair and watched Rafe deftly measure out the tea leaves. "Obviously you don't need a wife."

With a laugh, he switched on the stove. "Now, that sounds like a sexist remark, Doctor. Unusual coming from you. However, you're right. I don't plan to take a wife."

The statement was delivered in his usual laconic manner, but something in his tone indicated that he wanted his intentions made plain. His assumption that she was interested in snaring him irritated her.

"And I don't plan to take a husband."

"Oh?" He took a chair and turned it around to straddle it. "Why not?"

She smiled wryly. "I'm perfectly happy with my spinster status." That was putting it mildly. She felt a distaste for men in general. Oh, they were all right, but she found them totally unnecessary for her survival.

Rafe nodded, looking terribly pleased about this latest development. She was expecting him to make some kind of pass, but apparently curiosity won out for the moment. "Why are you starting practice so late?"

"You mean as an old maid?"

He had the good grace to flinch sheepishly. "You are a little older than most doctors just getting started, aren't you?"

"Poverty set me back," she answered honestly. "Every so often I would have to take a leave of absence from med school and work a term."

"Your parents couldn't help you out?"

"I didn't have parents, per se, Mr. Anaya." She tried to keep the bitterness from her voice. "My father came and went when the mood called. He had a certain charm. My mother was deeply in love with him and didn't have . . . whatever it took to put him out of her life forever."

"And your mother?"

"My mother was from Italy—a war bride. She died when I was sixteen."

She could have told him more—that her mother had spoken almost no English; that merely coping with a new language and new customs in the isolated oil fields had been a tremendous task for the shy, uneducated woman. And that the eldest of her nine children, a daughter who did speak English, had assumed that responsibility, though it meant months at a time when she hadn't gone to school. She could have told him that her mother had died young. From a hard life, too many pregnancies, or heartbreak? Mary didn't know.

She only knew she didn't want the yoke of marriage.

"I sort of get the feeling you're afraid of relationships with the opposite sex, Doctor."

His seriousness surprised her. "I have nothing left to fear, Mr. Anaya."

"You say 'Mr. Anaya' 'cause it makes you feel safe, doesn't it?" His eyes met hers with a challenge that rattled her all the way to the core.

Her stomach signaled another attack of heartburn. She tried to sound flip, insouciant. "It logically fol-

lows, then, that when you call me 'Doctor,' you seek
to think of me as without gender."

He smiled, and her stomach dropped. "I assure you
that I have never needed to think that. Now, I reckon
if I were to call you by your first name, you would
withdraw behind that cool, professional exterior. Can
you deny it, Mary? See what just happened? When I
used your name, your hazel eyes immediately deep-
ened to gray. A gray like the shade of desert juniper."

The conversation was getting dangerously out of
her control. "What about the tea? It's ready."

His eyes twinkled at her cowardice. "Of course."
He rose to pour the tea into two ceramic mugs. The
tea was as dark as coffee. "How did your trip to the
barrio go?"

She accepted the mug he passed her, hating the way
her breath caught at the touch of his fingers. "How
did you know I visited the *barrio?*"

"The people of the valley know everything that *la
soltera* does. Even now the word has gone out that
you're in my house alone with me." His eyes glinted
wickedly. "Do you realize that you may be compromising your spinster status? Does the prim, brisk,
efficient doctor have another side to her?"

Evading his question, she took a drink of the green
tea. "Agggh!" she said. "It does taste furry!"

His easy laughter could lull one into thinking that
he was actually relaxed. But she knew that was a
mistake. The charm might be on full, but she sensed
that his guard was never relaxed.

She set the cup down. "I wanted to talk to you

about the trip. The people live under very unsanitary conditions. A lot could be done to alleviate their illnesses if someone could explain to them about hygiene."

Her tea cooled as she became involved in talking. Rafe listened patiently, saying nothing. His eyes watched her, studied her, over his cup's rim, and she knew he was wondering about her.

Still, she plunged on. "Many of these people have never held a toothbrush, let alone seen a dentist. Why, I even saw an infant drinking water from a baby bottle that had silt in the bottom of it. Rafe"—she used his given name this time without thinking—"I know I could do so much to help these people if they weren't afraid of me. If you could take me to talk to the *curandera*—to Josefita—I would like to gain her friendship and acceptance. She could give me entrée to the people I could help."

He set aside the empty mug. "The people who live in rural, isolated areas live very close to the land, Mary. They aim to lead self-sufficient lives. With outsiders they're shy and reticent. I reckon some would say they're doubtful and suspicious."

"I'd have to say that," she sighed.

"You have to understand that they live in an intensely person-oriented society. They value independence and rely on their families for aid and support." His eyes demanded that her gaze meet his wholly. "I'm trying to tell you that trust must be built. It's not something that can be won overnight."

Exasperated, she cried out, "Then why did you apply for me?"

"We were hoping the doctor would want to stay."

"And I won't."

"We were expecting a male doctor."

"And I'm female."

"I'm very much aware of that."

She rose. "It's getting late. I'd better be going."

"I'll drive you back to your house."

"No, that's all right. I can walk back."

He eyed her with tolerant amusement. "Didn't anyone ever tell you that after evening has cooled the desert floor, tarantulas and coyotes and centipedes like to prowl around?"

It was her turn to smile. "And lecherous men. I grew up in the Southwest, Mr. Anaya. I'm not as much of an outsider as you think."

"But you are a spinster," he said, guiding her toward the front door. "And that does set you apart here."

Outside, a sliver of moon shone brightly, but the night air was already chilly, and she was grateful for the warmth of his pickup. She kept far to her side of the cab, listening to the distant mission bells.

"You know," he said, easily breaking her silence, "there is a legend about Kingdom Come's mission bells."

The moon's light was just bright enough that she could make out his face, but neither his expression nor his rich, accented voice gave her any clue as to whether he was teasing or not.

"The old-timers," he continued, "say that a couple of centuries ago a very wealthy *gachupín*, an *hacendado* of pure Spanish blood, donated the money for the mission's bells with the stipulation that, should his daughter request the marriage sacrament with her Indian lover, the padre was to refuse. When the *hacendado*'s daughter heard of the bargain she ran away from home to meet with her lover, but her father found the two of them before the hour was out. He had the Indian killed."

"I take it this is not going to end happily-ever-after like the fairy tales?"

"I'll let you be the judge. The bells arrived, and the padre was disgruntled to find that they had been so badly cast that they rang like a donkey's neigh rather than pealed like a song. The padre had the bells' ropes removed rather than let them ring.

"Meanwhile, the *hacendado* went ahead with his plans for his daughter's marriage to a local *hidalgo*. This time she ran away to a convent in Mexico City. She did not take the vows, for she considered herself married in the soul to her Indian lover. Years later she returned to die an old lady—a lonely spinster."

"I don't think I like your legend," Mary said crisply. "A spinster isn't necessarily lonely."

He halted the pickup in the shadow of her house and laid his arm across the back of the seat. "Ahh, but the story isn't over. By coincidence, the day of her death a new padre took over the mission. He ordered ropes attached to the bells. This time they pealed wildly, beautifully. The people who had known the *hacendado*'s daughter as a young woman swore that the bells were singing for the spinster, singing because she was at last with her Indian lover."

She wished she could see his face, could see if he were mocking her. She could think of nothing to say, and asked instead, "Will you take me to the *curandera?*"

"You are a persistent woman, Mary."

"Next week?"

She heard his laughter, rich and husky, just as she liked it. "Ahh, Mary!" Then he reached out and captured either side of her face, then pulled her to him.

"Oh!" she gasped. Shocked, she pressed her hands against his chest.

He brought her mouth to his. Beneath the mustache that softly rasped her skin, his lips were warm and soft and hotly arousing. His hands slid down to her hips, stroking, caressing, inching downward.

Thinking to escape, she pushed against him, but his arms wrapped tighter. "Mary . . . *querida,*" he whispered deliciously into her mouth, "I've been wanting to kiss you so badly."

She turned her head and said coolly, "But I don't want to kiss you."

His mouth, hot, moist, brushed her temple, pulsing with an excitement that entered her veins and moved through her blood. His lips buried themselves in her hair, and his breath fanned her ear. "Are you sure, honey?" he asked with enormous self-confidence.

Her lips opened to assure him, and she felt the

touch of his honeyed tongue. He entangled it with hers, and she felt like she was melting. She was achingly aroused. She muttered something—"Don't" . . . or maybe his name.

He let her draw away—only a couple of inches, so that he could make out her face. "Mary, honey, how about having dinner with me tomorrow night?"

"I'm busy."

"But not too busy to visit the *barrio?*" He sighed. He would take what he could get. He was a patient man. But not, it seemed, where Mary Margulies was concerned.

Why had he told her the story about the mission bells? It was a story that as a child he had loved to hear from his grandmother. The mystery, the majesty, of the story held something personal for him, though he couldn't say exactly why or what.

So why had he shared the story with this woman sitting beside him, who—however enchanting—was nonetheless a total stranger?

For a moment Mary thought she saw puzzlement displayed in Rafe's handsome features. Probably not. His kind were always certain of themselves. The puzzlement she thought she had seen was merely an illusion created by the dimness inside the pickup cab.

"If you want to be accepted by the *barrio* people," he said, as if the conversation had never been interrupted, as if he had not undergone the same appalling, sweet madness she had, "try wearing something less intimidating than a doctor's smock when I pick you up."

Chapter 4

"THANKS, VICENTE." MARY TOOK THE SACK OF FOOD, mostly canned goods, and smiled good-bye.

"Adiós, soltera."

The term no longer offended her; still, why couldn't the people think of her as a doctor?

She stepped outside into the bright sunlight to find a large man with broad shoulders sitting with one leg hooked over the fender of her Mustang. His weight lowered the car's front bumper by a foot. He had a build a linebacker would have envied. The dark green uniform, the brown Western hat, the highly polished boots and the .38-caliber pistol belted at his hip all proclaimed him to be a member of the Border Patrol.

He finished cleaning his opaque sunglasses and slid them over his heavy broken nose. "'Morning, little lady."

Some patients—children—she liked immediately, immensely. And some adults she detested immediately, immensely. This was one, though she had no idea why. But "mean" was spelled out in everything about him. "Good morning."

"Chief." He tipped the broad brim of his hat. "Chief Joe Hanson."

The sack was getting heavy. "Is there something I can do for you?"

"Little lady—"

"Doctor," she said frostily. "Dr. Margulies."

His thick lips slowly stretched in the imperturbable grin of a person who knows that he will ultimately have his way. "I represent the United States Border Patrol's meager attempt to stem the alien tide. In other words, keep the dirty Mexes out of the country."

Now she knew she didn't like him. "And?" she asked, not bothering to hide her impatience.

"Our drag trail shows us—"

"Drag trail?"

"Yes'm. We use four-wheelers equipped with drags to smooth out the ground's surface. That way, little . . . Doc, we can detect footprints or car tracks left by an illegal entrant. Even the approximate time a person crossed such a trail can be estimated. And as I was saying, we know that you were out driving in the area we keep under surveillance."

She walked past him and opened her car door. "But I am not an illegal alien . . . Sergeant Henley."

He slid to his feet and faced her. "Chief. Chief

Hanson. Just wanted to make sure you report any wetbacks you come across. And remind you that you aren't to render medical treatment to any of 'em."

She looked over the top of the car's door at him. "Let me remind you that according to the Hippocratic code it's my moral duty to render medical treatment to whomever, whenever."

He delivered a "good-ol'-boy" smile. "Sure, if you're a private citizen or a doctor with your own private practice. But you're working for the NHSC right now, Doc. That's a government organization. Therefore, you'd be breaking the law. Just as I'd be breaking the law if I helped one of them cockroaches. So, if you do treat a wetback, it'd be my most unhappy duty to arrest and jail you. Just thought I'd warn you, Doc."

She slipped behind the steering wheel and slammed the car door shut. Through the windshield she saw him tip his hat. "'Day, Doc," he called out.

From behind the bank's plate-glass window, the tall, mustached man wearing a battered Stetson watched the interchange between Hanson and Mary. Rafe's lips stretched flat. Hanson had been brought in because of the increase in illegal aliens. Dr. Mary Margulies was a person ripe for trouble, and Hanson would break her. He was a tough career man. Rafe had seen his kind in the Special Forces, men who had lost all sensitivity.

He had been afraid that the Special Forces had made him one of them. Until Mary. She had opened the floodgates of feeling. He was staggered by how badly he wanted to make love to her. He recalled her particular fragrance. She smelled like a delicate gardenia, a pale desert gardenia that haunted the twilight with its scent. And he remembered her breasts pressing into his chest, enticing mounds of creamy softness that parched his throat. But she held more for him than just a sexual attraction. And that worried him.

"Why the frown, honey?" Christina asked in her low, whispery voice.

Idly he looked down into the feline-sharp face framed by the sleekly waving blond mane. Her long, manicured nail rimmed the buckle of his belt suggestively. The marbled pillar and his tall frame concealed her seductive byplay. She was exciting in bed, but God help the man who got caught in her mercenary clutches.

Rafe knew full well that her interest in him ran further than his prowess at passion. Try three thousand acres, matched many times over by greenbacks and stocks, and a long line of aristocratic ancestors whose family name was still revered in El Paso's *haut monde*.

"Concern for our new doctor," he answered noncommittally.

Christina's Nordic blue eyes deserted his mouth to clamp on Mary's small figure, made even tinier by the Samson of a man who talked with her. "Think Hanson wants to get her in the sack?"

As Rafe looked down at her, he shook his head in bemusement. Christina was completely amoral, and despite his vast experience, something deep inside him winced at calculated crudity in a woman. His grandmother's error in raising him like she had, he thought with amused derision.

He experienced a sudden deep hunger for the soft warmth and tenderness of a woman. He recalled kissing Mary, and her sweet, innocent response. He could have gone on kissing her like that for hours. He had kissed hundreds of women, all shapes and sizes and colors, but he had never felt so good afterward, filled with an elusive kind of happiness. He missed the sweetness that came with anticipation. How long since he had been teased and tickled? How long since he had lost himself in the pure delight of laughter?

The six months the delectable little spinster was to spend in Kingdom Come might turn out to be a very pleasant, very special interlude after all—at least for him. For her, professionally, the outlook was dismal.

"Well, what do you think about the two?" Christina persisted. "The doctor and Hanson?"

He captured Christina's wandering beringed finger. "I think that you had better finish explaining this benefit idea of yours," he said huskily.

She made a monumental effort at self-control—an attribute she rarely needed to practice except with Rafe. With her sharp, feline instincts she sensed that he liked the challenge of the hunt, something that had always been her prerogative. The feminists of the world would never succeed in making a tame male of Rafe Anaya. His intrinsic masculinity was too firmly grounded in his Hispanic heritage, a heritage that proclaimed the male a very separate and distinct entity from the female in every way. And she thrilled to that dominating—but not domineering—masculinity.

She leaned her silk-sheathed body against the marbled column and stared up into the eyes that perused her with such interest. Good. Her father wanted a grandson *now*. And he made no secret of his admiration for Rafe's reputation with the women, nor his wish that she become a part of that reputation—with the blessings of the church, naturally.

She was tall for a woman, but Rafe was so much taller that she was forced to look up as she spoke. "I was just talking to Daddy about a benefit for our new clinic when I saw you enter. And it occurred to me that we could host it together. After all, the clinic was your idea. And a benefit would only be the proper thing for the Andersson clan to do for the community. Bjorn tells me that it doesn't have any laboratory or X-ray facilities. We could—"

"Your brother's been treated there?"

"Of course not, honey. If he had something wrong with him, he'd see someone really qualified."

Rafe raised a brow. "And Dr. Margulies isn't?"

Christina's full lips pouted. "Oh, you know what I mean. Honestly, Rafe!"

Sometimes, when he looked at her like that, she wondered if she'd ever be familiar with the intricate workings of his mind. He showed a complete lack of desire to conform to anyone's morals but his own. And she knew he could be ruthless when he decided on a course of action. The barren presence of the worthless *barrio* land along the river that he had prevented the City Council from acquiring and turning into a golf course attested to that relentlessness.

But it was the other side of him, the more primitive part of him, that interested her more. His wild passions brought her to a frenetic fulfillment that no other man could. His unrestrained, reckless lovemaking indicated youthful excesses and an endless succession of women. And she wanted to be the last of them.

"Miserable creep!" La Jean snapped. She spread the old magazines she had brought from home, *de rigueur* for a doctor's office, fanwise on the second-hand coffee table. "Eddie thinks that Hanson is the dregs of humanity."

"I can't imagine why," Mary said dryly. She sifted through the information forms needed for Social Security benefits. At that point it looked doubtful whether the clinic would ever have a patient to fill one out. She was irritated by the prejudice of the community.

And irritated at her emotional preoccupation with Rafe Anaya.

"How do you explain to someone that rheumatic fever can result from an untreated strep throat," she asked La Jean, "and drive home the fact that he could save fourteen dollars by coming in for a six-dollar throat culture instead of a twenty-eight-dollar office visit—especially when he lives on the dole anyway?"

"You don't." La Jean popped a stick of spearmint gum in her mouth. "Not when Josefita can treat him with a home remedy for next to nothing."

Mary slammed the sheaf of information forms on the reception desk, fluttering the papers. "And how does she treat cancer and silicosis and organic brain disease brought about by paint and solvent sniffing?"

La Jean grinned and shrugged. "You'd have to ask the old witch."

Mary's lips pressed in a grim line. "I plan to do just that."

"When you do—"

La Jean broke off as the front door opened and an Indian girl of perhaps sixteen slid inside, almost pressing herself against the wall. But no fear flickered in her dark eyes. Rather, there was a certain caution, a wariness, as if she were listening intently for some pursuer.

When a moment passed and nothing happened, she smiled triumphantly at the two gaping women. With her widely spaced teeth, square face and cropped hair, she was positively homely. Her wide feet wore worn huaraches, and a cheap cotton blouse and brightly colored skirt clothed her narrow-boned body.

Mary saw herself at that age, hiding her fear of society's policies, power and procedures behind a facade of bravado. But somehow that bravado had toughened her for life later. The bravado became, in fact, courage. In retrospect, she wouldn't change her life.

She stepped from behind the desk and crossed to

the girl. "I'm Dr. Margulies," she said gently. "Can I help you?"

The girl's shrewd eyes darted to La Jean, and Mary said, "La Jean is my assistant." Then, afraid the girl might not understand, she added, "She works for me."

The girl looked back to Mary. *"Estoy encinta."* At Mary's puzzled expression, the girl's work-roughened hand formed a mound above her stomach in the age-old gesture of pregnancy.

"I understand," Mary said. She motioned for the girl to follow her and talked softly, reassuringly, on the way down the hall. "While I check you, you can tell me everything."

The girl told her nothing. Her face was set in a mask of stoicism as Mary took her blood pressure to establish a baseline level, then examined her heart for function, rate and rhythm.

When Mary indicated that the girl needed to remove her clothing and don a disposable paper gown, the girl studied Mary before her lids drooped to conceal whatever expression might have been found in her eyes.

Mary touched her shoulder, wanting badly to establish a good rapport. "It's all right. I'll leave the room."

Outside, La Jean handed her an empty folder and mouthed gleefully, "Our first patient!"

"An awfully desperate one to submit herself to the discomfort of an examination," Mary said quietly. "Why?"

La Jean grinned, and her shoulders lifted in a characteristic shrug. "Maybe Josefita's overloaded with patients."

Mary rolled her eyes in feigned disgust.

When she reentered the examination room the girl sat on the table, her head downcast. Mary tried to make the examination as easy as possible, asking questions to distract the girl. Predictably, the uterus was slightly enlarged and somewhat softened, as was normal for pregnancy. She noted the position of the ovaries and the tubes. But the pelvic measurements did not bode well. Too narrow, but not unusual for a young girl in her first pregnancy.

Tactfully she turned her back while the girl scrambled to right herself and readjust the paper gown. Picking up the folder, Mary asked the preliminary questions—not actually expecting answers. "What is your name and how old are you?"

"My name is Hermalinda María Dolores Hernández. And I am sixteen years old."

So the girl understood more English than had been apparent. Mary wrote the name on the chart. Hermalinda. Ironically, in Spanish the name had something to do with being pretty—something this girl could never be called. Below the name Mary scribbled notations of the examination results.

She turned to face the girl and asked forthrightly, "Why have you come here instead of going to the *curandera*—Josefita?"

For a long moment Hermalinda said nothing, and Mary had the distinct feeling the girl was sizing her up. Then, in badly accented English, Hermalinda said, "I live on the other side of the Rio Bravo. The Rio Grande, you call it. In El Porvenir. I come to you because it is the best possible gift—to give my *bebé* the chance to be an American citizen. Josefita cannot give me these papers. A doctor with those"—she pointed to the diplomas on the wall—"a doctor can give me the papers that make my *bebé* a real American."

"I see." She saw only too well. Like Hermalinda, she had once faced what seemed a hostile world and insurmountable obstacles. All of her family had. She thought of Michael, in prison. Why did some people, facing the same adversities, succeed, where others didn't?

The Indian girl interrupted her introspection. "I want you to deliver my *bebé*—to give it American citizenship."

Mary knew that as a government employee she could lose her license to practice and even face possible prosecution if she were actually caught administering treatment to an illegal alien. At least, that was how the United States Border Patrol felt about the situation. She doubted it would ever come to the loss of her license, but it could jeopardize her chances with Scott-Waggoner.

Still, they would have to actually catch her in the act. And merely observing a pregnant alien didn't constitute an illegality. Hanson would have to catch her dispensing medicine or delivering a child. And of course, that she wouldn't do. She would never break the law. Nor would she be so foolish as to jeopardize a promising career with a prestigious clinic.

She smiled at the scrappy girl, who watched her closely. "Your baby is due in a little more than six months. It is best for your baby's health that you come back here for checkups. Every month. Do you understand?"

The girl nodded, her homely face visibly lightening.

"But I will not deliver your baby, Hermalinda."

The gapped teeth showed in a smile of certainty, and Mary had to blink at the smile's uncanny resemblance to that of Hanson. The same unflappable smile that announced that ultimately its owner would have her way.

Hermalinda cocked her head. "You are what the *vendadores*—the street people—call an easy touch, I think."

Mary snapped the folder closed. "I wouldn't count on it, Hermalinda. You better understand now that, just like you, I am street-wise. You're dealing with someone who knows every game in the book."

The same imperturbable smile. "We will see."

Mary rolled her eyes, feeling her patience slip away in the face of the plucky girl's persistence. Taking several pharmaceutical samples from the glass cabinet, she handed them to Hermalinda. "These are prenatal vitamins. It's important for your baby's health that you take them. One every day."

The girl held the vitamin bottles as if they were

precious jewels. Surprising Mary, she grasped her
hand to plant a childish kiss on its back. *"Gracias . . .
soltera."*

Mary repressed a groan of exasperation at the
inescapable sobriquet.

With no patients—or patience—forthcoming, Mary
left the clinic at four o'clock to finish the unpacking
that had been delayed by the need to finish setting up
the clinic. Clad in pink-striped running shorts and a
solid pink tank top, she was ready to unpack the
remaining sheets and bath towels, keepsakes and
pictures of her brothers and sisters.

She had set her beloved Dieffenbachias and Schef-
flera and English ivy about the rooms to personalize
the place. She did this everywhere she lived, trying to
make the places into the home she never had. "You
know," she said aloud, talking to the plants as she
worked, "I'm just beginning to adjust to this little
adobe. Almost."

If she could discount the garish green-and-purple
upholstered furniture.

"Of course, there are scorpions and tarantulas,"
she muttered as she put away her medical textbooks.
But then, how many homes had front yards shaded
with exotic fruit trees and windows bowered with gay
bougainvillea?

She was discovering that the border region of Texas
was a land unto itself; a desert that with irrigation
became a semitropical land of fiesta and flowers; a

romantic land of moonlit patios, muted guitars and the music of soft Spanish vowels.

Doubled over the edge of an almost empty packing box, only her rear end visible, she was startled by the softly Spanish-accented voice behind her. "A presentation of your better side?"

She floundered upright. Rafe stood outside the kitchen's screen door, thumbs hooked in his jeans pockets and a bawdy grin on his face. Instantly she tugged the shorts down over her derriere's curves. "Peeping Tom!" she muttered.

His chuckle sent her stomach on a wild roller-coaster ride. She had never before considered that laughter could be seductive.

His mustache twitched at her obvious discomposure. "May I come in?"

Her survival instincts told her no. This man was dangerously different from all the other men she had met. His kiss had vastly altered her in some indefinable way. Something in her had been changed forever by that kiss. She had ceded something—what, she did not know—to him, and she felt terribly vulnerable, as if she had been caught almost naked.

Of course, she had.

"All right, come in," she said, more than a little ungraciously.

He let himself inside to stand, hands on hips, grinning down at her. He wore tan jeans and a cream-brown chambray shirt that emphasized his yellow-brown mustache. In the shadow of his Stetson's brim, his eyes twinkled irrepressibly. Was it possible for eyes to be that shade of brown—almost golden?

"Who were you talking to?" he asked with a puzzled look around the room.

Her nose tilted. "Why, the plants. It's good for their health."

"Speaking as a doctor, of course?" he teased.

"Of course." She wasn't going to give ground. If only he weren't so disturbingly attractive.

With a long, appraising look, his eyes ran up her small, nicely rounded body to settle on her hair, carelessly massed in a knot at the back of her head, several tendrils escaping down her neck to wisp about her tender alabaster nape.

A blush invaded the narrow V of her breasts and marched up her neck and cheeks to pinken her delicate shell-like ears. Her freckles washed out beneath that wave of color. She knew he wanted her. How could she not know when his manner was so candid—and so terribly appealing?

"You needed something?" she asked.

"You don't by any chance have any tea, Doctor?"

What she had was heartburn.

Minute explosions detonated in her stomach and rippled like earthquake tremors through her body, touching the furthest corners, electrifying every nerve ending. She had no experience by which to judge the sensual attraction between a particular man and a particular woman, an attraction that went beyond logical explanation. Neither her virginal body nor her virginal mind had ever been touched by love or passion, and she felt a panicky need to escape.

"I have orange pekoe," she said with an attempt at dignity. "Will that do?"

He pushed his hat back. The buttercup curls were dampened by the sweat band. "What I'd really like is green tea. But I reckon we can pick up a package on the way to Josefita's. Vicente keeps a supply in stock for me."

"You're taking me to the *curandera?*"

The ends of his mustache dipped with his grimace. "Against my better judgment."

"Let me change into some jeans," she said, and quickly turned to leave before he could alter his decision to take her.

During the rough, jouncing ride to Josefita's, Rafe told her about *curanderas*. "They view illness in a religious and social context, not in the medical-scientific one of Anglo society. The *curanderas* rely on herbs and *remedios*. And their rituals probably have enough herbal and psychological benefits to work, sort of by restoring the mental and physical balance of the body."

"Rituals?" Mary snapped. "Remedies? What you're talking about is witchcraft."

Rafe wheeled the pickup down a dirt road that led toward the green ribbon of the Rio Grande. "Not at all, though a *curandera* is sought when a person is thought to be *embrujada*—bewitched. The *curandera* puts great faith in God to contribute to the cures. Both she and the patient know that God put these remedies on earth for this purpose—what we call miracle cures."

Mary almost snorted her contempt. "Does she know how and when to order tests and interpret diagnostic laboratory studies?"

He flicked her a look of tolerant amusement. "As a doctor, you should know that many prescription medicines are made from herbs. And that chemicals are added which affect people. Those chemicals aren't natural, and can often do more harm than good."

"I think I'm seeing the primitive part of you."

He kept his gaze trained on the corduroy road. "It's always just below the surface, Mary. In all of us."

She was enjoying this intellectual exchange—something she had certainly not expected from the community's playboy. She studied his rakishly handsome profile. The muscles in his forearms below his rolled-up sleeves were taut, controlling the vibrating wheel of the bouncing vehicle. For just a moment she experienced a surge of some wild, reckless emotion that made her want to cast off all the years of carefully established caution and feel those arms about her, straining her against him.

The urge was a painful ache inside her, and she crushed it by attacking. "Let me tell you about one of the *barrio* houses I visited. A home remedy—the mother told me it was a brew known as sheep-dip tea—was given to her year-old son to make him break out in hives. She honestly believed the hives were in the child and had to come out. Naturally, since children are allergic to the tea, he did get hives."

He shrugged. "There is the other side of the coin. A buddy in El Paso—we met in Argentina—credits a medicine man for effectively controlling malaria he picked up in Nam. When he followed the treatment of medical doctors, he said, he suffered attacks about once a month. Now he's down to one a year, an improvement which he credits to the herbs prescribed by the shaman."

She and Rafe were at an impasse on the subject. Regrettably, before the merits and drawbacks of another issue could be argued, they arrived at Josefita's. The *curandera*'s home was located on a narrow dirt road that paralleled the river's bank. A large grouping of trees flanked the sagging shack, giving it a lush garden effect, and a junk car lent inspiration to the front yard.

Mary got out of the pickup quickly, before he could come around to her side. Once again she could almost feel the heat of his gaze sliding down the length of her.

"You're lovely, Mary."

"Don't."

His lips curved in a warm smile that most women rarely saw. "I must say, I find your jeans less exciting than that first state of dress—or undress—I caught you in."

She stifled an inward groan. Would he never let her forget? And yet she sensed in his teasing humor . . . What? Affection? Surely not.

A little woman, smaller even than herself, came outside to greet them. She wore a blue leaf-patterned dress and, incredibly in that heat, a black sweater.

Her face was leathery, her dark gray hair caught stringently in a bun at her nape, and her nose was hooked. Yet her wise old eyes were almost beautiful. And guarded.

"Josefita," Rafe said, "this is Kingdom Come's new doctor, Mary Margulies."

The old woman nodded, holding herself with the immense dignity of the old-world *hidalgos*. Her carriage, her expression, said that she was no mere peon but a *doña* of great respectability.

"I'm happy to meet you, Josefita."

"I have been expecting your visit," the old woman said simply.

Mary arched a delicately delineated brow at Rafe, and he shrugged.

They followed her inside the shack, which wasn't in much better condition than the outside. Bullfight posters, serving in place of wallpaper, peeled from the walls. The floor was covered with cracked linoleum, and the sparse furniture was of cheap, badly hewn pine. But the house was clean, though it reeked of cooked cabbage, fish and other, indistinguishable odors.

The *curandera* settled her small-boned frame in a creaky rocker. At that moment a slight woman with waist-length ebony hair and a pure olive complexion came to stand at the kitchen door. Her gaudy red-flowered skirt and cotton peasant blouse could not detract from her fragile good looks. Yet her eyes held a serene strength, and Mary knew that the young woman was the *curandera*'s daughter even before the older woman introduced her.

The daughter, Carmelita, nodded shyly, but her gaze lingered on Rafe, and Mary sensed they were old friends. He said something in Spanish, laughing, but with the same warmth that Mary had felt earlier.

Carmelita smiled joyously and replied. So he affected all women the same way.

Behind Carmelita a boy of perhaps five or six poked his head into the room to better view Mary; then, gathering courage, he went to stand at the old woman's side. Clad only in a pair of red shorts, he was barefoot—and badly cross-eyed. "My grandson, Lucero," the old *curandera* said.

Rafe settled a thigh on the broad armrest of a bench across from Josefita. Following his example, Mary took a seat near him on the smoothly worn bench, saying, "I would like to help your people, Josefita. I have been trained in new ways to cure their illnesses."

No emotion showed in the woman's face. "Our ways are good enough. My mother passed on her methods to me. I will pass them on to my daughter. It has been done this way for generations."

The woman's obstinacy nettled Mary. "But I have been able to learn things that are new even to today's doctors."

The old woman fixed her with a basilisk gaze and said nothing.

"Are you afraid I will steal your patients?" Mary asked.

Josefita lifted shoulders that had been slightly stooped by time. "They know I will not treat them if they go to you."

Mary strove to retain her cool. The visit was obviously going to be a short one. With what dignity she could muster, she rose to her feet. "We shall see," she said, and only then realized that she was parroting Hermalinda.

Josefita levered herself from the rocker to face Mary. Her eyes, hooded with time's wrinkles, flashed. But Rafe came between her and Mary. His hand took Mary's elbow, and tiny shocks sparked through her again. "This discussion is best postponed," he told the two women.

"*Adiós,* Josefita," he said at the door.

"Rafael?" the old woman said.

"*Sí?*"

She rattled off something in rapid-fire Spanish, and he laughed.

Once he and Mary were in the pickup, she asked what the *curandera* had said.

He grinned and backed the pickup out onto the dirt road that was shadowed by the evening's lingering light. "She said to tell you to try *yerba buena* for your stomach ailment."

"How did she know I had stomach problems?"

"I don't imagine it was too difficult. Isn't that part and parcel with the demands on a busy physician?"

"Except I'm not busy," Mary said tonelessly.

"Then how about getting a bite to eat with me at the Oasis?"

Her head shot up. "Well, no . . . I can't," she said stiffly. "Really, I'm too busy."

His golden-flecked eyes danced mischievously, and humor lurked in his voice. "I thought you just said you weren't busy?"

"I meant that I . . ." How could he get her so flustered? She was cool, composed Mary Margulies. "It's just that I have a lot of unpacking still to do at home. I'm sorry."

"Don't you read the paper? I'm the most eligible bachelor in town."

"Really?"

Piqued, he drove across the stone bridge to park before the adobe. "Good night, Mary," he said evenly. He would be damned if he would humble himself.

Bleakly he watched her scramble from the pickup as if she were in jeopardy of losing her life—or maybe her virtue. Or both.

What was he supposed to do with the rest of the evening—go home and tumble into bed? There was the High Lonesome, where female companionship could always be found. Yet at that moment any woman paled beside Mary and the ripeness of her curving hips and the tantalizing gardenia scent that lingered in the pickup. And those pixie's freckles that unaccountably aroused him. The memory of her soft lips coiled hotly through him, and he nearly groaned in disgust at his weakness for Dr. Mary Margulies.

Chapter 5

"FIFTY DOLLARS," MARY SAID, GIVING THE BANK TELLER the information he needed to make out the money order. It was for Billy. He had written in response to her invitation to visit her that he could escape the Permian Basin's oil fields over the Labor Day weekend. It would be the first weekend the rig crew he worked with would get off. The money was to pay his bus fare, since his rattletrap car was broken down.

Labor Day was still a long way off—there was still the Fourth of July to go—but she wanted to make certain that Billy came.

"Dr. Margulies?"

Mary turned, money order in hand, to face the nice-looking man in the three-piece pin-striped suit. She judged him to be about her age—and to be the possessor of a very engaging smile. He stuck out his hand. "I'm Beau Brewster, the Valley Bank's vice-president."

She shook his hand with a firm grasp. Beau Brewster. She recalled La Jean mentioning him as being one good-looking and very available guy. La Jean was right, as usual.

Beau, the bank's newest vice-president, had been hired away the year before from a large Dallas banking firm with nine vice-presidents too many. La Jean had claimed that the trio made up of him and Rafe and her Eddie contained the town's most sought-after men. Not that Beau shared with Rafe and Eddie the camaraderie of the Three Musketeers.

"I know that you're new in town," Beau said, "and I know just how you feel. I've only been here about a year myself, and the place takes some getting used to."

She returned his smile. Here, at last, was someone who could understand the loneliness she felt in this desert wilderness. "It certainly does. I had forgotten what isolation really means."

"Almost the same as being quarantined, I suppose."

"Worse," she said.

"Look," he said in a genial voice, "I know you've been invited to the benefit for your clinic that the Anderssons' are having. Why don't I pick you up—say, around seven tomorrow night?"

Smooth. She recognized that kind. Smoother even than Rafe, but not quite as intriguing. Maybe she was just getting crotchety in her old age. "I don't think so,

Beau. I don't know when I'll be able to get away from the clinic. I'll see you there," she compromised.

"Just because a community is remote doesn't mean it isn't bustling," Father John said, his blue eyes twinkling as they swept the Anderssons' crowded solarium which, with its enclosed pool, was almost as large as a convention hall.

For the fifty-dollar-a-plate benefit dinner that night, candlelit tables had been strategically placed both inside the sumptuously appointed solarium and outside on the brick patio. A hired mariachi band strolled among the guests, softly playing romantic songs, and houseboys in loose white cotton *camisas* and *calzones* plied Kingdom Come's elite with trays of wine and champagne and calorie-filled hors d'oeuvres.

Mary felt as out-of-place there as a fat matador would feel in the bullring.

And she was surprisingly grateful for Beau's presence. She returned his inviting grin. Why not? With dark brown hair, blown dry in a perfect style, and those clear blue eyes, he was a very attractive man. Bright and enterprising, he had not let two divorces embitter him against the fairer sex.

His manner was slow and subtle, unlike that of Rafe, who would hustle her right into his bed—if he should be lucky enough to live so long.

The fact that Beau was much more restrained in his approach suited her quite nicely. However, the three-piece suit he wore did not lull her into believing he was a staid businessman. His eyes, veiled by incredibly long lashes, played hopscotch over the milk-white skin exposed by her wraparound black dress. The frilly white band that edged the neckline's deep V made the dress—and her bosom—spectacular.

"Want another cocktail?" he asked when Father John was captured by a plump matron interested in saving her brother-in-law's soul.

Mary shook her head and handed him her half-empty glass. She wasn't about to entrust her sobriety to a businessman who had more than business on his mind.

Undeterred, he took her glass and wove his way through the maze of guests to the nearest houseboy to have his own glass refilled.

Her gaze deserted Beau's back to slide over the people in the room. All well-to-do farmers and ranchers and businessmen, more than eager to contribute to the clinic. But not eager enough to come to it. Of the hundred or so guests, maybe a handful had dropped by with emergency complaints, and a handful of patients was not enough to maintain the clinic satisfactorily. Furthermore, those few whom she had treated had still been reserved and distant, though polite, when they left.

Regardless of the fact that she wanted to serve their community, she was still an outsider. "A spinster," she had overheard whispered behind hands more than once that evening.

Her gaze fell on Rafe, who was talking to Christina and the thin, nervous Bjorn. The Andersson scion was neither as fair as his sister nor as dynamic-looking. Neither was his wife, Nelda, with her Shirley Temple sausage curls that seemed to bounce on hidden springs.

Christina wore a frothy chiffon dress of pale blue beaded with silver that accented her Scandinavian beauty. In comparison Mary thought her own dress was drab and colorless. But it was the only cocktail dress she possessed.

Involuntarily her gaze kept returning to Rafe. With the roguish butter-yellow mustache, he was elegantly sexy in a Giorgio Armani silk suit, making Bjorn seem pallid beside him. Whether wearing a silk suit or old jeans and boots, Rafe exuded a steamy aura. Still, he looked definitely restless, uncomfortable in the rich apparel. His tie was already loosened and his vest open. His expression stated that he was clearly bored.

At her side, Father John said, "An interesting man, isn't he—Rafael?"

"Everyone here is," she replied diplomatically.

She wanted to feel Rafe's mustache tickling her neck. She felt a heated blush steal over her. Thinking back to the trip she had made with him to the *barrio*, she couldn't remember one word of his explanation about *curanderas*, but she meltingly recalled every personal word they had uttered, his husky laughter, the way her stomach did somersaults at his touch on her bare arm.

"But Rafael is somehow different, I suspect," Father John continued. "He gives the impression of being laid-back, with his easy laugh and remarkable ability to tell a good story, doesn't he?"

Rafe's story of the *hacendado*'s spinster daughter and the miracle of the bells, she thought ruefully, confirmed the priest's opinion. "You might say that, Father John," she hedged.

"Yet behind that front, my daughter, is a street-smart organizer with a political savvy acquired in countless battles with bureaucrats, police, aldermen, mayors and real-estate tycoons. He presides over our community board like King Solomon at his court."

Squarely she met Father John's placid gaze. "Do I detect a matchmaker in Saint Tomás's padre?"

The old man's eyes widened innocently. "My daughter, would I interfere with the Master's omniscient plans?"

Her merry laughter slipped out. "I think you would offer up plenty of suggestions to Him."

"I am," he said, his seamed cheeks dimpling roguishly. "I am."

Christina moved about the cliques of people, graciously dispensing her charms. Nelda Andersson trailed in the socialite's footsteps. Mary thought that Christina masked her enjoyment in a pose of contemptuous tolerance, especially when Christina deigned to speak with her for a few patronizing moments. "You look . . . so nice, Dr. Margulies." Her glance was disparaging.

Nelda nodded. "Yes . . . so nice."

"Thank you. You look . . . like you've taken good care of of yourself, Miss Anderson."

The woman's artfully plucked brows shot up, and

Mary added with a smile, "Health-wise, speaking from a doctor's point of view, of course."

Following cocktails, Lars Andersson officiously lent his presence to the table at which Mary sat. Besides being an astute businessman, the barrel-chested man was an entertaining host, incorrigibly optimistic, with a Santa Claus laugh and an effusive nature.

"Don't you mind none, Dr. Margulies." He patted her hand in a not-so-paternal gesture, and she caught the black scowl Rafe directed at Andersson from the next table over. "We'll have that clinic packed with an impressive array of medical equipment in no time at all."

"I would prefer to have it packed with patients, Mr. Andersson."

The man attacked his food. "Oh, that. Well, don't you mind that none, either, Dr. Margulies. Eventually the clientele will build."

But how long was "eventually"?

Later she courteously thanked the Anderssons for the evening, all the while irritated at their social snobbery. The clinic was worth supporting publicly, but not good enough for them to patronize. With Rafe, whom she at that moment considered one of "them," she allowed her lips to curl in a scornful smile and coolly made her gracious good-bye.

She left the Southern-plantation-style mansion along with the other guests, who, loosened by the socializing—and the drinks—were laughing rowdily as they drifted out to their cars.

Even though Beau had escorted her to her car, she

felt a sudden terrible loneliness. A poignant longing.
When she opened her car door, Beau's arm promptly
curved about her waist and his head snuggled against
her neck. Apparently he, too, had tipped one too
many glasses. Deftly she stepped out of his embrace
and slid behind the wheel.

"You not interested in men?" he asked, genuinely
puzzled.

"Not interested in sex."

A pained expression flickered over his face, but she
knew he would continue to make passes. Men who
had made it to a vice-presidency rarely gave up—on
anything. Neither did the Rafe Anayas of the world.
Particularly the Rafe Anayas.

On the drive back she thought about the loneliness
that squirmed within her. It was something she hadn't
experienced since . . . since she was a child and
walked the street at four in the morning because there
was nowhere to go and nothing to do. Analyzing the
peculiar loneliness she was feeling, she knew that
during dinner she had been constantly aware of Rafe's
casual, supremely male interest in her, though he had
addressed her only once the entire time.

Yet all evening she had tingled beneath the heat
from his golden eyes. Now, released from that pinning
gaze, she felt almost disoriented, jangled, lacking
interest in anything.

She parked her car in the lee of the adobe's lime
trees and leaned against the steering wheel, letting the
sense of desolation drain through her body. When she
got out, headlights flashed over her. Rafe, driving the

white MG, pulled up beside her car. He slid from behind the wheel, unfolding his length to look down at her. His tie hung loosely, and he was in his shirtsleeves. She clutched at her purse, feeling that panicky need to escape all over again. Despite the rich trappings, he was a Mexican *bandido* come to steal a night of love.

He braced his hand against the Mustang, near her shoulder, and his gold cufflink reflected the light of the moon-dusted night. "You didn't like tonight?"

She looked beyond him, unable to meet the eyes that consumed her with such refined lust. A thousand stars studded the black velvet sky, seeming so close there on the high desert that one could almost reach up and touch them. "I enjoyed myself."

"Did the banker boy kiss you good night?" he growled, irritated at what he recognized could be a formidable rival.

Her gaze snapped back to his. "That's none of your business." But her own jealousy of Christina Andersson prompted her to ask, "Did you have a good time?"

"No. All the while I was wishing I was somewhere else. With you."

"Rafe, why do you want to be with me? I won't go to bed with you."

"The hell if I know why," he muttered.

Abruptly his hands caught her shoulders, and he drew her against him. His touch had an incendiary effect on her. Her hands grasped at the crisp linen shirt. Then he kissed her, with such a thoroughness, and for such a long time, that a small, moist ache began between her legs. Never once did he attempt to part her lips. He simply memorized their shape with his own. It was the first time, she thought dazedly, that a man had ever made love to her mouth. The effect was cataclysmic.

He set her from him, and she missed the sweet wine taste of his mouth. "I won't lie, Mary. I want to take you to bed. Badly, dammit."

Her laughter was soft, low, her smile the equivalent of a dismissing shrug. "Then find someone else to take to bed. Because I'll only be here a matter of months. And I don't intend to have a casual fling."

His hand captured her heart-shaped little chin, tilting it upward. "It won't be a casual fling, I promise you. I'll abide by your rules, but I warn you that I intend to change your mind, Dr. Mary Margulies."

Then he kissed her again, roughly this time, as if in retaliation for her rejection of him.

Bemused, she watched the MG spin away. His reckless all-or-nothing seduction had excited her. True, her stomach was churning with that old gnawing. But now there was also that insidiously sweet ache between her legs.

Rafe sprawled diagonally across the enormous bed that had been in the family for generations. He had been born in that bed. The elaborately carved headboard and footboard had been hewn by expert Mexican craftsmen from the finest rosewood, as had been most of the furniture in the *hacienda*'s five bedrooms.

Hands behind his head, he scowled at the ceiling that was inset with scrolled molding. From the high-boy the television blared out the late news. But he wasn't listening. Three times in the past two weeks he had called Mary at the clinic to ask her for a date. No go. Too busy.

Not too busy, however, to have lunch with Beau Brewster at the Oasis that afternoon. Rafe's male ego was beginning to show bruises. He was mad as hell. And just thinking about the way the skirt she had worn hugged her lush little bottom made his tempera-ture go up ten degrees more.

"Hell!" he muttered, and rolled to his feet to turn off the television.

He strode into the bathroom, discarding his jeans, shirt, and navy briefs in a trail behind him. A cold shower would solve the monstrous ache throbbing in him. A cold shower or a hot woman. But he didn't want any of the women whose names filled his private address book. Names with faces he couldn't remem-ber at that moment. Only one face presented itself, hauntingly clear. A lovely face with a sweet, innocent mouth and large eyes that laughed when they weren't wary.

He didn't know how long he soaped in the shower, not really aware of the cold needle spray that pelted his lean body. All he could think of was Mary Margulies. Dr. Mary Margulies. She was more power-ful than the *curandera*. She had bewitched him.

He turned off the water and toweled himself dry. What did he know about Mary? Very little. That she was very intelligent and worked like an ant; that she most likely came from a broken home and had never been married; that there was nothing contrived or shopworn or studied about her. She was a warm, caring woman—with an impudently curved little rear. And she didn't play around. The startled O of her mouth after he had kissed her that first night had made that quite obvious.

One kiss and he was beguiled, bemused—and utterly bewitched.

"Hell," he muttered again, and prowled naked back to the double-arched window. Down the road a small light from the adobe quarters gleamed faintly through the lace of lime branches. It wasn't like him to go round and round a problem like a dog chasing its tail. When he decided on something, he pursued it until he got it.

But he obviously wasn't getting Mary Margulies.

In his younger years he had seen too much dissipation, too much debauchery. Wealth, good looks, a superior education and an aristocratic background had left him nothing to strive for. No goal in life. Jaded, he had found that the dangers of wealth were too hard to withstand. The temptation to lie back and enjoy his privileges had been well-nigh irresistible.

Vietnam and the Army's Special Forces had given him a glimpse of redemption. A challenge. Only the men of the best physical and mental caliber were accepted in the Special Forces. The elite organization demanded a tremendous amount of inventiveness and self-reliance. He learned to deal with special combat situations that weren't found in a textbook. He found himself in situations that, after Nam, took him all over the globe, involving him in the internal affairs of shaky countries.

Each man in the Special Forces became a specialist in Operations, Intelligence, Demolition or Weapons. Or Assassination. At that point, or somewhere in the haze of time that followed, he had found out that he wasn't the man for the task. He knew that for him there had to be a better way to save humanity from itself.

He had found a deep sense of satisfaction in returning to the soil. Rancho Encantado supported itself on its cotton harvests so that he didn't have to touch a penny of the stocks and bonds and trusts that were distributed in banks throughout the Southwest and Mexico.

But even Rancho Encantado had not fully occupied him. He was restive. With his BS in agronomy he found time several mornings a week to instruct his people on how to increase productivity while maintaining the environment and making the most efficient use of the soil and water.

He thought he was beginning to establish a worthwhile pattern to his life, with occasional affairs with sensational women to tantalize his spare hours. Every once in a while he thought about marriage to whatever women was at that moment holding his fancy—until boredom invaded again.

Then Mary had showed up. Mary, with that proud walk and imperious tilt of her chin—and that lush little body that she had so charmingly displayed for him in the closet with the water heater. Now he was keyed-up and high in his heat, but wanting something more than just sex.

Mary stood, arms akimbo, and glared down at the flat tire. She didn't know the first thing about changing a tire. Rather than identify lug nuts and tire-jack positions, she had memorized arteries and fetal positions. With a sigh she opened the trunk, and dust flurried over her white doctor's smock. She pulled out the jack that looked as foreign to her as a bronchoscope would to an auto mechanic.

The lug wrench she could handle. She sat on her heels before the flat tire and began unscrewing the lugs, which required more strength than she would have thought.

"¿Soltera?"

Surprise almost caused her to jerk a lug nut off. She looked up to see a stooped old man in pajamalike clothing. In his hand he held a peaked straw sombrero. His leathery face was as wrinkled and brown as the Texas badlands. He pointed in the direction of the nearest field. "You want, I ask *el patrón* to send you help?"

She glanced in the direction he pointed, toward the nearest field. A group of men were hunkered down in a semicircle before Rafe, who was easily identifiable by the drooping yellow mustache. He was crumbling the soil in his hand as he talked. *El patrón,* the old Mexican had called Rafe. The protector. Grudgingly she had to admit that he was that—at least to his people. He worked side by side with them, cared about them, looked after them.

Funny, all her life she had protected others, her mother, her brothers and sisters. Now, to have someone like Rafe want to protect her . . . It was something her soul had always yearned for and that had been denied her. Yet she didn't think protecting her was exactly what Rafe had in mind. "I think I can manage by myself, *señor*," she told the old man.

He nodded his head with a gumless grin and ambled away. She went back to wrenching the lug nuts loose until a shadow fell over the Mustang's fender. She looked up to find Rafe standing over her. Tall, self-confident, handsome, he was looking at her with amusement that somehow didn't mock her faltering attempt at changing the tire. Instead she thought she saw something akin to admiration in his expression.

"I realize you're an emancipated woman and all, Mary, but could I help? Next time I'm sick, you could treat me for free," he added with a lopsided smile before she could reject his offer. "We'd be even."

Slowly she nodded her assent. Rising, she dusted off her hands while he removed his plaid cotton shirt and hunched down before the tire. The bright sunlight picked out the muscles that bunched across his bronzed shoulders and revealed puckered white flesh that must have been the remains of an old wound. Watching him work rapidly and deftly, she felt a breathlessness that surely had to do with the dry heat. With all that sky, there simply wasn't any air in it.

Within minutes the spare tire had replaced the flat one, and he was standing beside her, shrugging into his shirt. Dirt was smeared in a path across the arrogant line of his nose. "Mary, are you still too busy to see me?"

"Of course not—if it's a professional consultation you're seeking," she quickly qualified.

His mouth flattened so that it was a grim line beneath the shadow of his mustache. "I'm seeking the woman—not the doctor."

Feeling cornered, she bit out, "Rafe, you accused me of not wanting to establish a relationship with the opposite sex. But you don't want to establish a *lasting* relationship with the opposite sex. One is just as bad as the other."

His smile was roguish. "Then let's console each other."

She expelled a breath of impatience. "Consolation isn't what I need. Thank you very much for your help." She swept past him and slid behind the steering wheel. When she glanced in the rearview mirror he was still standing there, watching her drive away. Frustration was etched into his expression.

An hour later, when Mary entered the clinic, La Jean was bent over, busily scribbling on a file chart, her orange hair her only visible feature. "Don't tell me," Mary said dryly. "We had so many patients that you had to turn them all away until later in the week."

La Jean looked up, and Mary saw concern in the usually sparkling eyes. "Two, as a matter of fact."

"Oh, no, I missed them!" Mary braced one hip on

the edge of the receptionist's desk, loosening the hem of her powder-blue shirtwaist dress when it snagged on the splintered wood. "First I had a flat. Then I dropped off the baby food and medicine and milk formula at the Ruizes'."

"Does the baby have jaundice?"

"I don't know. The mother wouldn't let me in."

La Jean's lips curled downward. "You would have fared just as well—or as badly—had you been here instead."

"Do I want to hear this?"

"Hermalinda came by for her monthly checkup. She was afraid to wait."

Mary sighed. "Her progress should be monitored." Did the Indian girl wade across the Rio Grande? And how would she manage when she grew larger with child?

"It gets worse. Your other prospective patient was an older woman who brought her son in for an examination. I don't know what his ailment was, but she told me her husband had threatened to beat her up if she came to see you. You know, the old *machismo* bit. Anyway, she was also afraid to wait."

Mary's small fist slammed against her thigh. "I'm going to conquer the ignorance that leads to such tragedies if it's the last thing I do in Kingdom Come."

"It may well be," La Jean said with a wry grimace. Then, when Mary slid to her feet, she asked, "Where are you going now?"

"Back to Josefita's. If you can't beat them, join them."

La Jean looked askance at her, as if she were suspicious of her employer's sanity.

So did Josefita when Mary appeared at her door. But the old woman invited her inside. Carmelita was nowhere to be seen, but the grandson Lucero clung to the old woman's skirts. He was a beautiful child, Mary thought, like his mother, with lustrous black curls and honey skin. Except for the crossed eyes. Did he never play with the other children?

She seated herself again on the worn wooden bench and began speaking earnestly, desperately. "Josefita, I think you and I can learn so much from each other. I want you to let me go with you when you treat your patients."

Josefita fixed her with a single eye. For what seemed a long time there was no movement in the little house. At last Josefita said in a raspy old voice, "I will let you go with me, but never, never—are you to interfere. I cannot promise that the people will let you into their homes. There are many who think you are a quack, a fake—the same things that you think of me."

Mary sensed that the old woman hoped the hostility of the *barrio* people would discourage her interest in remaining in Kingdom Come for the full six months. But she had never been one to get discouraged easily. "I understand."

Yet Mary saw much that day that she did *not* understand.

Like herself, Josefita carried a bag with the tools of her trade—some protective charms, including religious medals, red ribbon, little sacks containing herb mixtures to be worn around the neck. The two women, with Lucero in tow, walked to the other *jacales*. The sun was hot, the wind was hot and the sand that wedged in Mary's sandals was hot.

At the first *jacal* a young man suffered from headaches, mystical visions and a lack of appetite. Mary saw visual proofs of his affliction. Josefita diagnosed the disease as *mal ojo*—the evil eye—and recommended wearing pink coral and said a prayer.

At another house she diagnosed the old man as having *cólico*—colic—and proceeded to rub his bloated stomach with a fresh egg in the sign of the cross, reciting the Apostles' Creed three times. At that same house the old man's great-granddaughter wanted to look in Josefita's bag for the babies that she thought the old woman delivered in her capacity as a *partera,* or midwife.

At each of Josefita's calls the people eyed Mary with suspicion, the same suspicion which must have shown in her own eyes as she watched Josefita work. However, she saw evidence that Josefita was in many cases administering superbly to the people's ailments. Often the *curandera* distributed herbs that were the basis for many modern medicines: crushed *osha* from the parsley family for headache or toothache; lavender as a sedative and antiseptic; *manzanilla* for female troubles; horehound for coughs; raw *ajo,* or garlic, to be taken internally for controlling high blood pressure.

That afternoon Mary made the return drive to her adobe, brooding over what she had witnessed but hopeful that perhaps she had made progress in getting the *curandera* and the people of the *barrio* to accept her.

Her slightly lifted spirits evaporated when she looked in the rearview mirror to find the Border Patrol's green four-wheeler bearing down on her Mustang. The four-wheeler nosed alongside her car, and Hanson motioned for her to pull over. Seething, she edged the Mustang onto the shoulder. When she rolled down her window, fiery dry heat shimmering off the hot tarred pavement seared her face and burned all the way down to her lungs.

Hanson parked behind her and lumbered over to brace his beefy hands on the window ledge. Sunlight scattered off the reflective lenses of his sunglasses. "'Afternoon, Doc."

The slug. "You wanted something, Sergeant?"

His thick lips folded in a slow smile. "Chief, ma'am."

She eyed him frostily and said nothing. She had the greatest urge to roll the window up on those piano-key-sized fingers.

"Just wanted to tell you we picked up a pregnant little greaser. Right after she left your clinic."

Mary's heart thudded. At times La Jean had related Eddie's comments about Hanson. Those tales of the man's cruelty with captured aliens slammed against Mary's brain. Since then she had heard mutterings of all sorts of physical abuse—beatings, robberies, a gunshot victim found dead with signs of having been handcuffed. Worse, Beau had once hinted that women sometimes had to submit to sex with Hanson as the price of not being returned to Mexico.

"What did you do with her?" she asked, almost afraid of the answer.

He took off his hat and wiped his sweaty forehead with the back of his sleeve. The hat's contours had molded his hair into a misshapen mass. "You weren't treating the little greaser, were you, Doc?"

"What did you do with her?" she demanded again, a slow hot anger building in her at this repugnant representative of the human race.

"I interrogated her." He shrugged his mooselike shoulders. "Then I followed SOP. Standard operating procedure. Put her on a bus to El Paso's detention center to await deportation hearings. But by next week the little hot tamale will be at it again, stealing across the border."

Mary smiled and said sweetly, "Did you ever hear, 'Give me your tired, your poor, your huddled masses yearning to breathe free'?"

His eyes, hooded by the low forehead, looked at her, puzzled.

"I doubt that you're well read enough to know that that's the inscription on the pedestal of the Statue of Liberty. But surely you recall Jesus' words, 'When I was hungry, you gave me food; when naked, you clothed me; when a stranger, you took me in'?"

Then, with malicious delight, she shoved the car into drive and peeled off, spraying gravel and dusting the border patrolman.

Chapter 6

SLOWLY MARY CAME AWAKE. AT FIRST SHE THOUGHT IT
had been the unpleasant dream she had been having,
compliments of Chief Joe Hanson, that had awakened
her. The sheets clung stickily to her thighs and
breasts. Never having had pajamas or nightgowns as a
child, by the time she was an adult she had acquired
the habit of sleeping in the raw. Well, almost, if the
simple nylon briefs were discounted. But now even
the lacy briefs adhered damply to her flesh. From the
window, moonlight dusted her alabaster breasts,
sheened with perspiration.

She sat up and pushed back the tangle of russet hair
that was wet about her nape and temples. When
released from its knot the dark red-brown hair draped
all the way to the small of her back in a wildly curling,
perpetually tousled mane. She found its heavy, unruly

length particularly burdensome in the desert heat, but she could do so many things with her hair when it was long. And besides, it was her one concession to her femininity in a profession dominated by men.

Her digital alarm clock glowed the hour of three-twenty-seven. She wiped her hand down her breasts' narrow valley where the perspiration trickled and tried to orient herself. Then she realized what had awakened her. The evaporative water cooler's hypnotic hum had ceased, which explained the stifling heat.

She struggled from the entwining sheets and padded into the living room, blindly circumventing the rustic Mexican pine furniture with its shocking purple-and-green upholstery. A little more brilliance and the cushions could have glowed in the dark like runway lights.

She flipped on the lamp and balefully eyed the water cooler that sat silently in the window, stolidly defying her to repair it.

"Damn!"

She could perform an emergency cesarean, but she didn't know the first thing about mechanical apparatus. She went through the house, throwing on lights, until she reached the circuit-breaker panel in the utility closet. The water cooler's switch functioned properly. So much for her one attempt at repair.

By midmorning, with a temperature of a hundred-and-five-plus, the adobe would be hotter than an oven.

Muttering further imprecations, she returned to the

living room to stand, hands on hips, and glare at the unresponsive water cooler. Blossoms of blue jacaranda and pink bougainvillea gathered along the ledge of the window adjacent to it, pervading the living room with their intoxicating sweetness.

Down the moonlit road the windows of Rafe's *hacienda* were darkened. The thought of him sleeping while she sweltered annoyed her. The thought of *him* annoyed her, period. And unfortunately she knew why. It was because she was thinking about what it would be like to lose herself in the purely hedonistic pleasure of his kisses. To her great misfortune she enjoyed those kisses very much. Too much.

What did he sleep in? Pajamas? No. Briefs? Maybe. Most likely in the raw. At the mental picture heat washed over her, though she was already sweltering.

She was tempted to telephone him; after all, he was her landlord and responsible for the adobe's maintenance. But she recalled all too well his warning that he wanted her in his bed. She wasn't ready for something like that. Maybe later, once she had established her practice—hopefully at the Scott-Waggoner Medical Complex in Washington. Maybe then she would be ready for an emotional envolement.

Except she was already emotionally involved. She found him exciting and enjoyed being around him; she respected him for his deep commitment to his people and for his integrity, an integrity which prompted him to admit that he wanted no lasting relationships—and that he wanted her in his bed. At no point had he tried to delude her. He had been completely honest.

Good sense told her to wait until morning to notify him about the water cooler. It would be better if he repaired it when she wasn't there. Cursing her logical, practical nature, she crossed the room to turn out the light—until the heavy rap on the front door halted her. She froze beside the deep tufted armchair. "Who is it?" she managed to call out through lips suddenly gone useless.

"Mary . . . it's Rafe. I saw your lights on as I drove by. Are you all right?"

She glanced down at herself. Naked again. Or almost. "Just a moment."

She hurried back to the bedroom and grabbed the only robe she had, a graduation gift from Amy and Billy. She had always considered the champagne-colored satiny wrap too sinfully expensive for practicality. Mary Margulies, Princess of Practicality.

Tying the ribbon sash about her waist, she returned to the living room and opened the door. No doubt about it, filling the doorway was Rafe with that sweet, lascivious gleam in those pale brown eyes. Beneath the swath of golden mustache his mouth donned its rakish smile. He wore white slacks and a paprika-colored knitted shirt that begged her fingertips to stroke its sleek contours.

"Yes?" she asked with the greatest aplomb.

His gaze perused the room behind her, taking in the multitude of potted plants she had set about, then moved back to settle on her. He inventoried her length from the riotous mass of hair down past the pert, inviting little breasts to the toenails, beautifully pink with polish, that peeked from beneath the robe.

"Ahhh, Mary," he growled softly, "you look good enough to eat."

Her blush blew her composure. Stiffly she stepped back, holding the door open for him to enter. "At this time of night—or morning—I'm not interested in your flirtation."

His arms went around her waist, and he bent his head to nuzzle her neck. "Mary, Mary, quite contrary, why do you keep saying no?"

As low as she felt, his warm humor was still able to make her smile. "Now, you stop that, Rafe Anaya."

"Stop what, sweet?" he asked with all the innocence of a ferocious fox as his mouth, redolent of rotgut whiskey, or maybe *aguardiente*, pursued the twitching corner of hers.

She retreated a step and backed into the sofa's arm. "Ohhh, Rafe!" she cried out as she toppled over it to sprawl on the cushions in what looked like an obvious display of wild, wanton abandon.

"You do want me!" he said in triumph.

But when she rubbed her head with another "Ohhh" that was not a startled exclamation but a painful groan, he came instantly to her side, drawing her up into his lap. "Where does it hurt?" he asked, his fingers feeling gingerly over her scalp.

"There, just at the base. I hit . . ."

From behind her his hand produced the offending object. "A potted plant."

"Oh, no!" she moaned, eyeing the crumpled avocado leaves. That evening she had transplanted the burgeoning plant from a glass jar to the small ceramic pot, and had left the pot on the sofa when a back issue of *Modern Medicine* had caught her eye.

"You didn't need it anyway, honey," he consoled her, and set the battered plant on the cigarette-burned and knife-notched coffee table. "You spend too much time with plants and not enough time with me."

"I do not!" She rubbed her head gingerly. "Plants are much safer. They don't try to seduce me."

"Ahh, but they do attack. See—look at the knot on your head." At the way his fingers massaged the base of her skull—in almost a sensual ritual—she was beginning to feel a distinct lack of oxygen.

He pulled her back into the custody of his arms. "And besides, your plants don't make you feel all good and glowing inside, Dr. Margulies."

His foraging mouth belied his formality of address and gave her little opportunity to protest his statement. He kissed her playfully, gently, at first. Then the kiss changed to one of rapacious, greedy hunger.

"Ahh, Mary," he whispered against her lips, his breath hot, his eyes feverish with excitement. "You don't know the effect you have on my good intentions. I look at you and start thinking of a hundred things I'd like to do to you. Just thinking about you . . . Let me love you, honey."

"Rafe, no . . . please . . . don't." She was trying to think lucidly, but she was frightened, mostly of her own response. She was tired, worried, aroused. Foolishly, tears came to her eyes.

"Mary, honey," Rafe said, drawing back, "what is it? I'll stop . . . I'm sorry. But, by the saints, Mary, I want you so badly."

"It's not just you." She hiccuped and buried her face in the hollow of his shoulder. His after-shave was a heady stimulant. "So much has gone wrong this week. The cooler just went out . . . only two patients came in and I missed both of them . . . Hanson pulled me over just to harass—"

"That son of a—"

She pressed his lips with her fingers, smiling through her checked tears at the snarl that curled them. She had felt good, sharing with someone. It had been so long since she had let her guard down like that.

"Don't cry, Mary," he intoned, and stroked her hair absently, abstractedly. He got uneasy when women cried. And this woman affected him even more than most. "Please, don't cry," he almost begged.

"It's all right, Rafe." She managed a teary smile. "The Mustang buried Hanson in dust when I peeled away."

His snarl became a deep chuckle. "Why, Mary, I do believe Kingdom Come is beginning to corrupt your prim-and-proper ways."

He started kissing her all over again, this time using his warm, wet tongue to persuade her to part her lips.

"I'm not corrupted that much," she tried to tell him, but he was kissing her all over her face—on her lids, below the line of her jaw, on her chin, at the corner of her mouth, in her mouth again. The excitement built in her like a kettledrum crescendo, and her breath came shallow and fast as if it were she who was fleeing the relentless pursuit of *la migra*. She could hear Rafe's own breathing, labored and ragged, mingling with hers.

Traitorously her hands inched over his shoulders. She should have bitten her tongue, but it had a will of its own as it coupled in delicious combat with Rafe's. His large hands rounded about her bottom's curves, pulling her against him. That little moist ache between her legs demanded assaugement. With a shuddering sigh she squeezed her thighs together to forestall herself from revealing her arousal to the enemy.

Encouraged, Rafe pressed her down against the couch's cushions, his hand clasping her satin-sheathed breast, and half-covered her body with his heavier one. She attempted a halfhearted protest, but his mouth was silencing hers. And his kiss . . . If he didn't stop soon her bones would dissolve into hot fluid. She was sliding along the razor edge of sensuality.

"Mary, I want to be inside you so bad it hurts. Don't you like this?" He was rabidly kissing the exposed valley of her breasts.

"Rafe, you've got to stop. No"—she pushed at his shoulders—"listen to me, please!"

"Ahh, honey . . ." His hand somehow entangled

itself beneath her robe to cup one turgid breast. "I'll stop. But you know you want this as much as I do."

Yes. Yes! The kneading fingers. Oh, holy Moses! "No. *No!*"

He sat up and ran his fingers through his rumpled hair. His eyes, a puzzled expression in their smoky brown depths, scanned her closed face. "You . . . Mary, you're not the teasing kind?"

Embarrassed, she tugged together the lace edges of the gaping robe. Her lips wore that crushed-peaches look that said she had been thoroughly kissed. "No. It's not that." Her raspy throat wouldn't work properly. "It's . . . I'm still . . ."

Enlightenment dawned on his face. His brows lifted. "You're a . . . virgin, Mary?"

Her lips broke into a wan smile at the unintentional play on words.

"Come here, honey." His hands cupped her shoulders and drew her to a sitting position so he could cuddle her in the alcove of one arm.

"Rafe . . ." Her mouth pressed together in a tight little line. "Oh, Rafe, why can't we just go on kissing?"

"You can't be serious? In the name of St. Anthony, you don't think nature designed us to function only to a certain point? Mary, I can't hold back when I'm around you. I don't want to hold back. Kissing you is sweet torment, it's a lovely passion, but I want to show you how incredibly pleasurable lovemaking can—"

She tensed and extricated herself from his encircling arms. "Then you'll just have to stop seeing me."

The soft but simple reply struck him like a blow, taking his breath with a hurting force. "I'll play by your rules, then," he groaned. "Until I can convince you otherwise." He pulled her to her feet. "In the meantime, I'm afraid the cold showers I'll have to take are going to shrivel my skin so badly it'll be three inches too short for my frame."

She grinned saucily then. Standing on tiptoe, she splayed her hands on his chest for balance and kissed his beard-shadowed jaw. "I won't tempt you further."

"You already are," he growled, and removed her hands from his chest. "How about fixing some tea while I try to find out what's wrong with the cooler?"

She wrinkled her nose in distaste. "I don't have any green tea."

"You'd better begin stocking it," he tossed over his shoulder as he headed for the offending piece of machinery, "because I plan to spend quite a lot of time here."

When Mary saw Angelita Vargas sitting in the clinic's waiting room with her son Tranquilito pinned down in a seat on one side of her, she forgot her preoccupation with Rafe—and the fact that he was getting closer to her than she had ever allowed a man to come before.

"This is the lady I was telling you came by last week while you were out," La Jean explained, her lively eyes communicating that this was the same woman who had been afraid to wait around because of her husband's threat.

Angelita wore a tentative expression on her moon-shaped face. Behind that tentativeness, Mary felt, was hope that the woman doctor wouldn't do any harm to her child. Tranquilito, who looked to be about six or seven, was clean and his clothes presentable. The plump woman was obviously proud of the little boy.

Mary immediately knew the depth of the mother's caring, and she liked that. What she didn't like was the bruise smudged beneath Angelita's left cheek-bone. And another on one dimpled upper arm.

Tranquilito Vargas looked up when Mary approached. "Hello," she said, squatting down so that she was at eye level with the child. "I'm Dr. Mar-gulies."

"*La soltera,*" Tranquilito said. By now Mary had given up trying to get people to stop calling her by that name.

Tranquilito had a crooked grin on his face which seemed to start at one ear and run raggedly around to the other. His expression was a bit tentative, too, but the force of his warmth and openness was just as palpable. With curly brown hair and steady brown eyes, he came across as the kind of kid she liked immensely. He reminded her of Michael as a little boy. Did he still wear that engaging grin or had poverty, life on the wrong side of the tracks and a prison cell altered it into a sour, bleak expression?

Realizing that an examination room might be too intimidating for the mother and son, she decided to interview the two in the waiting room. La Jean tactfully disappeared into the back room.

Tranquilito wriggled delightfully while Mary, pulling up a chair, talked with the mother.

"My Tranquilito is a very good boy," the mother praised. "He makes good grades at Santo Tomás Parochial, *gracias a Dios,* and he helps me with his two younger sisters."

Her son grinned and flushed with pleasure to hear himself extolled like that. But then he turned a little purplish around the edges when his mother began to talk about his problem—bed-wetting.

"His sisters, they share a bed and they don't wet. Tranquilito—he has his own room . . . and a single bed that he wets every night."

Annoyance mixed with frustration crept into the mother's tone. "In the morning, after he eats breakfast, he goes off to school on the bus his father drives. Meanwhile, I have to pack water from the canal to fill the washing machine, all the time keeping an eye on his two sisters. Then—every day—I have to strip the wet bed and wash the wet shorts."

Mary knew that Tranquilito could be perfectly normal but be late in developing bladder control—often traceable in the history of one of the parents. She could treat the enuresis with a drug, but she preferred not to. Instead she tried the obvious first. "Let's turn this thing over to Tranquilito. He's a big fellow, and he's embarrassed about bed-wetting, so he wants it to stop."

Eyes downcast beneath a fan of sweeping lashes, Tranquilito nodded.

"And you're a little bit annoyed about it, too," Mary addressed the mother now, "and want the bed-wetting to stop. Why don't you try getting Tranquilito up early enough in the morning so that he can pack the water from the canal? He can put the water and his wet shorts and sheets in the washing machine himself."

Angelita wouldn't meet Mary's gaze. The woman kept looking to the side and down at the floor, so Mary knew there was something else, another problem, one Angelita hadn't mentioned yet. "What is it, Angelita?"

The woman sat there wringing her plump hands. Then she began to talk in broken sentences that tumbled from her cupid's-bow mouth for twenty minutes. *"Mi esposo*—my husband—he is a very proud man. This bed-wetting—it is not *machismo*. He did not want me to come here."

Mary knew then the explanation for the bruises.

"Fernando—*mi esposo*—he doesn't want for all to know about his son's bed-wetting. Before, I have had Tranquilito change his sheets—carry the water. But, no, Fernando, he insisted I do it myself, because soon all will know about Tranquilito's bed-wetting." She shrugged her ample shoulders. "Even now he will be very angry if he finds out that I come to the clinic. What can I do?"

Mary would have liked to run further tests, though

the clinic didn't have the facilities yet. She could send the samples off to El Paso, but she doubted that Angelita would have the courage to flout her husband and consent to the tests. At least, not at the moment.

"For the present, Angelita, why don't you try giving Tranquilito extra salt before bedtime. Maybe a large salty pretzel or a tortilla. Tests have shown that the salt prevents fluid from passing freely from the blood vessels into the kidneys."

"But then, *soltera*, he will be thirsty."

"Not really. It takes about an hour before thirst sets in, and by that time a child is usually asleep. Also, you might have Tranquilito go as long as possible during the day without urinating. There's been some success in stretching the bladder, but it may take a while. And, of course," she admonished, rising to her feet, "don't let him drink anything before bedtime." She ruffled Tranquilito's curly hair. "Come back and visit me in three or four weeks, so I can check Tranquilito's progress."

And maybe by then she would have made progress of her own with the people in the valley.

It was a Fourth of July party. Eddie was throwing it, and Mary had agreed to go with Rafe. She had nothing to wear but her old standby—the black wrap-around cocktail dress. Its chiffon material did drift about her like midnight mist and laid bare her slender arms and the upper halves of her creamy breasts. That afternoon, as she bathed and washed her hair, the anticipation of the party fizzed through her veins like heady champagne.

But now she was regretting her agreement. As was Rafe. Obviously.

Dressed in navy-blue slacks and a pale blue shirt that played up his golden-brown hair and mustache, he sat behind the MG's steering wheel, his mouth flat, his eyes a cold, hard brown. She sat as mute as a mummy against the far door, which wasn't far enough.

She knew what was wrong, of course. In between the day he had called her for the date and the moment he had picked her up, he had regretted the promise she had extracted from him before she would agree to go—No Seduction Attempts. Doubtless he felt like a castrated bull. And the Rafe Anayas of the world didn't like having terms dictated to them. Pleasure with a capital P had been denied him. Sometimes she thought men had only one thing on their minds.

What had happened to the shared laughter, the sparkling repartee, the intelligent conversations the two of them had shared? Was that all a woman was to him—the source of his sexual pleasure?

The night was headed for disaster, and both Mary and Rafe just wanted to get through with it, go home and write the other one off as a loss, the night as a mistake not to be repeated.

Eddie greeted them at the door of his large ranch-style home, directing a cheerful lust-filled grin at her stunning dress. Behind him the stereo blared disco music that could not quite drown out the conversations and laughter of the two dozen or so guests.

"I was beginning to believe he was going to keep his discovery all to himself," Eddie said with a wink of genuine enjoyment at taunting his friend. "I'm Eddie Williams—and you're gorgeous!"

In spite of her blue funk, she had to laugh. Eddie was so downright open. His eyes twinkled with sheer devilment, and his hair looked as if he had been enjoying a three-day romp in bed.

"That's enough," Rafe growled, and steered her past the amused host. "You've got your own woman."

The party was swinging, and La Jean, her head a ball of orange fluff above the rest of the guests', made her way through the pack to Mary and Rafe. "Thought you'd never get here," she said, and passed them glasses of frothy margaritas. "You're the star guest, Mary, kid—everyone is eager to meet Kingdom Come's lady doctor."

Mary had to smile. "I'm glad you didn't say 'spinster,' La Jean."

Eddie nibbled La Jean's ear with impudent naughtiness and announced that he would make the introductions. But Rafe, not trusting even his own friend with his prized possession, guarded Mary closely as they were led into a den crowded with more people, either dancing frenetically or leaning comfortably in corners and talking with lively gestures. The dining table, cocktail tables, end tables and kitchen were overflowing with all sorts of delicious concoctions contributed by the guests, and the liquor flowed freely. A magnificently good time was obviously in progress.

Eddie was famous for his parties. They enlivened his regimented professional life with the Border Patrol. With a rather nice inheritance to set him up for life, it was a wonder to many that he bothered to work at all—except for those like Rafe, who understood that driving need to do something worthwhile.

Rafe firmly squelched Eddie's bantering challenge that, as the host, he should be the one to take Mary around for introductions, and himself guided her through the rooms, introducing her to everyone: Malcolm, the curator of the town's small history museum, whose wealth of local knowledge absolutely fascinated her; Barbara, the barber; Ethel, the lawyer's wife, whose vitriolic tongue kept the group in stitches; Big Al, a railroad man who looked like a cuddly Saint Bernard.

All of them readily accepted her. But with all of them she sensed the unspoken question: to just what extent did her involvement go with the community's most eligible and well-liked bachelor? She parried their subtle investigations with an expertise that had stood her in good stead all those years in college, and in the process charmed everyone—including Rafe.

Watching her interact with his friends, he was forced to admit that she was more special than any woman he had ever dated. The warmth and caring she demonstrated for all classes of people; her fierce spirit, as evidenced by her tackling of Hanson, when most people feared the border agent; her lively intelligence; and those sudden sparks of impishness that could reduce the professional woman to an adorable child-woman . . . God, but he was about to lose his head over Mary Margulies.

The arrival of Beau Brewster, who had come in late with Christina Andersson and Bjorn and his Shirley Temple wife, Nelda, jerked Rafe back to reality. Especially when Mary greeted Beau just as warmly as she would greet Rafe himself. He was furious that he was allowing Mary to get to him. Turning his back on the charmed group that encircled her, he focused his attention on whatever point it was W. H. Delbert, Kingdom Come's one lawyer, was trying to make, the man's plump forefinger jabbing the air like a striking snake.

Christina took one look at Mary, surrounded by Rafe's friends, whom she was enchanting with her mixture of wittiness, gaiety, shyness and utter warmth, and then the Scandinavian beauty dismissed the spinster as a sheer plebeian. A common little thing with common little freckles and blessed with a figure that really did curve too much.

Unconsciously Christina's hands smoothed over the apricot sheath where it hugged her almost nonexistent hips. Her lips curled ever so slightly, and she deserted Beau, who seemed mesmerized by Mary, to go in search of Rafe, whom she found deep in conversation with W. H. Delbert.

Whatever fireworks had been planned for the Fourth of July celebration could have been eclipsed by the blaze in Mary's eyes when the stereo launched into a slow romantic tune and Christina draped her svelte body over Rafe's to begin a slow, sinuous dance.

When Rafe finally got around to dancing with Mary, toward the end of the evening, she was as stiff as a board. He made an effort to relieve the situation, but his heart wasn't in it. No doubt she would have been just as happy dancing with Beau or W. H. Delbert, as pompous as the man was.

"You look beautiful tonight, Mary."

"Thank you."

"Eddie mixes great drinks."

"Yes, he does."

He gave up and feasted his eyes on her gorgeous figure. After all, wasn't this what she wanted? To be left untouched, pure as the driven sand? Where had that sweet, warm woman gone to? And why couldn't she be willing?

The ride back to Mary's house was awkward, silent, dull. When he escorted her to the door, both of them were relieved when, with a minimum of pleasantries, he discharged his duty to see her inside and she shut the door.

The following week the clinic received a visit of a different sort—from whom, Mary was not quite certain. She and La Jean both happened to drive up that morning at the same time. Neither of them had brought up the taboo subjects of Eddie's party and Rafe all that week. But Mary sometimes caught sympathy for her plight in La Jean's marvelously round eyes.

"I don't believe it!" La Jean said first when Mary unlocked the door and opened it.

Mary stood in the doorway, dismayed at the sight before her. Medical texts, file folders, office supplies, magazines—everything had been taken from the desk and shelves and strewn over the floor. A statue of a mother balancing her son on her knee, a gift from a fellow student, had been smashed.

La Jean moved about the room picking up objects. "Maybe one of your patients wasn't happy with his bill."

Mary didn't have the heart to smile. She headed for the examination rooms. Someone after drugs was her first thought. Both rooms looked like a *cantina* at closing time. Glass was shattered; bottles and packets had been flung from one wall to the other. Fortunately, none of the medical equipment, for which the Anderssons' benefit dinner had paid, had arrived. But the damage was still depressing.

Shards of glass framed the doors of the cabinets in which pharmaceutical samples were kept. But later, when La Jean and Mary made a careful inventory, it became obvious that nothing was missing. Apparently it had been an act of pure vandalism.

La Jean paused in sweeping up the broken glass. Her jaws were working overtime on her ever-present gum. "Why? Why would someone do this? And who?"

Mary continued to restore the samples to the

cabinet shelves. Her mouth was set in a grim line. "I don't know. Too many people don't want me here."

"Are you going to notify the authorities?"

"No."

"Are you out of your mind, Mary? It might not be the clinic that gets it next time. It might be your body!"

Mary slumped down in one of the waiting room's chairs and tilted her head back, closing her eyes. "I don't think so. If the anger had been directed at me, whoever it was would have chosen to ransack my house, not the clinic."

La Jean threw up her hands. "You're either awfully naive or awfully brave."

"All right," Mary sighed. "I'll file a report, for all the good it will do."

Chapter 7

It was almost closing time when Rafe opened the clinic's door. La Jean looked up from the Medicare form she was typing. Despite her growing love for the irascible Eddie, she could still fully appreciate the sight of Rafe Anaya and enjoy the secret fantasies daydreamed by women all over the valley and undoubtedly quite a few women up El Paso way.

Six feet, three inches of pantherish grace, Rafe Anaya's spectacular good looks were saved from the effete handsomeness of a male model only because he was so lustily, ruggedly masculine. And one thing she could say about him, he didn't take his wealth seriously. Sex, yes. Legends of his fantastic virility were widespread.

He wore dusty denims and a white workshirt that accentuated his bronzed skin. The shirt was only partially buttoned, and its sleeves were rolled to his elbows against the day's heat. Perspiration glistened in the golden hair that spread across his chest.

Did the mustache tickle when he kissed Mary? Mary would never admit to it; she hadn't even mentioned the rogue's name in the weeks since Eddie's party. But Eddie indicated that Rafe was suffering withdrawal symptoms and was prone to make nocturnal forages past the adobe.

"'Afternoon, Rafe," she said cheerily. "What can I do for you?"

He removed his battered Stetson and wiped the back of his arm across his sweaty forehead. "Mary in?"

La Jean's long, narrow face lit up with interest. Maybe there was hope after all! Maybe Rafe would even take care of Mary Margulies' marital state.

But, no, La Jean rejected that scenario. He was as much committed to his "playboy-after-dark" status as Mary was her spinsterhood. It must be business that brought him. "Mary's at the high-school rodeo." The mischievousness in her made her add, "With Beau Brewster."

The golden ring around Rafe's brown irises flared. "What the hell is she doing there with him?"

"Why, she's donated her time to care for any injuries," La Jean evaded with an innocent expression.

Rafe jammed his Stetson low on his forehead. "She certainly doesn't need a banker to help her administer first aid."

La Jean smiled sweetly, triumphantly. "I think she told me that she had never been to a rodeo and that Beau used to make the rodeo circuit as a teenager. So he's showing her the ropes, so to speak. And of course, it's a civic duty he's performing."

"Beau throws more bull around than the rodeo contestants do!" Rafe growled.

He growled to himself on the drive back to Rancho Encantado. Mary would readily see Beau, but was wary of himself. Her fawnlike shyness with him made him extremely uncomfortable. He had always considered himself a relatively tender man. But sometimes . . . sometimes she brought out his savage male lust. He felt the need to destroy something—beginning with Beau Brewster.

Rafe's pride was dented, his male confidence a little rattled. He was as frustrated as hell. Mary was becoming an obsession with him. Why, he didn't know. She wasn't his type at all. Too intellectual for what he had in mind.

But that wasn't true. He liked everything about her. He was trying like the devil to control himself— and it galled him bitterly that he didn't seem able to.

The few times he had been around Mary since the party, he had restrained his desire—well, as much as was possible for him. And with her so near at hand . . .

A few times he had stopped in, ostensibly to perform a few repairs on the old adobe, and one time just for coffee—she still hadn't taken him up on his suggestion of stocking green tea. On those rare visits he had failed to induce her to surrender even one of those stingily guarded kisses. Rather, she had seemed inordinately occupied with watering her plants or dusting them or talking to them—whatever one did with plants.

He hated himself for practically begging, something new to him. But, oh, just the memory of the enchanting and dangerously sensual shape of her mouth, the memory of exploring the warm wetness of those kisses . . . that honeyed tongue . . . and a liquid heat coiled through him. This sweet anticipation was practically causing him an ulcer.

He was aware of several intense urges, the most vital one being to feel himself buried inside her. After his possession of Mary Margulies—Dr. Mary Margulies—then this nagging misery would be ended.

What he needed was another woman, a woman with the divine gift of lechery. No, what he needed was Mary. But she didn't want him.

Her combination of sensuality and childlike innocence created a mystique he was committed to unraveling—if she would ever let him get close enough. Surely she couldn't maintain that cool composure constantly. But whenever the powerful urge to hold her close overcame him, a warning would creep into her eyes, and he could literally feel her draw away, as if she had unseen antennae that picked up the urges that periodically overcame him—the urge to hustle her off to an island in the middle of the Rio

Grande. Well, maybe a sandbar. Even her couch would do.

Maybe Mary's stomach ailment was contagious.

He intended to exile himself in the office for the rest of the evening and catch up on the ranch's mound of paperwork. He was determined to take his mind off a spirited little creature with merry hazel-gray eyes and red-brown hair that curled riotously despite her stringent efforts to tame it.

Near eleven o'clock his foreman interrupted him. Manuel stood at the library's patio door, turning his peaked sombrero between his hands nervously. He was a man of medium age and height with a wiry build and a swarthy, pocked complexion—and was totally committed to his *patrón*.

"¿Sí, Manuel?"

"*Patrón*, there has been an accident."

It wasn't like Manuel to be so reticent. Apparently this accident was different from most. Rafe began buttoning his loose shirt and tucking it inside his jeans. "What kind? Where?"

"A shooting. *La migra* ambushed a *mojado*. I was checking the east floodgate when I saw the headlights flashing along the river road."

Rafe started out the office door with Manuel following. "The wetback—did the Border Patrol arrest him?"

"No, *patrón*. *La migra* laughed and shouted in Spanish, 'Come out immediately. I've seen you.' Nothing moved. Then the same voice repeated,

'Don't play games with me, 'cause it'll be worse for you. Come out now, or I'll make you come out with bullets.' After twenty or thirty seconds I hear three shots. Maybe ten seconds later I hear the *mojado* splashing through the water. Then *la migra*'s spotlight picked him up on the far side. I see him collapse on the bank. I hide in the willows along the river and wait for *la migra* to drive away. *El mojado,* he is wounded, I think."

Rafe strode toward the pickup. "Get the floodlight from the barn," he ordered over his shoulder. "I'll swing by for you on the way back from *la soltera*'s."

When Mary opened the door Rafe felt like he had run into a brick wall. She wore that same gold satiny affair that clung to her pert little breasts. She blinked sleepily, pushing the disheveled curls back from her face, and he regretted that he couldn't take advantage of her sleepy confusion to seduce her back into her bed. A futile thought, for her eyes quickly cleared, widening with that ever-present wariness.

"What is it?" she asked in a voice still husky with sleep.

"There's been a shooting. The Border Patrol winged an illegal alien who had just forded the river."

She drew the robe around her tighter, defeating her own purpose, for those delectable nipples were clearly contoured by the satiny fabric. He managed to lift his hungry gaze to see the conflicting emotions pass across her lovely face. "Rafe, if he's an illegal alien . . . How badly hurt is he?"

"I don't know. He collapsed on the Mexican side of the Rio Grande—outside the jurisdiction of the United States government."

She was already leaving the room. "Let me throw something on."

He repressed the ungentlemanly urge to follow her back to her bedroom and feast his eyes. His gaze traveled over the room, personalized by her warm touches. The potted plants, the throw pillows, the scattered magazines, the upended wooden crates of books. He'd have to see to it that bookshelves were built. But then, she had already informed him that she wasn't planning on staying in Kingdom Come.

"I'm ready," she said from the doorway.

With time so short, she hadn't bothered with her hair but let it have its own way. She was dressed in a T-shirt stenciled with "NEW MEXICO STATE UNIVERSITY" and faded jeans that positively hugged her lush rear, exactly what he wanted to do at that moment.

"Your bag?"

"It's in the trunk of my car."

"We'll take the pickup," he said, propelling her out the door. "The terrain along the river is rough, almost inaccessible."

He took her car keys and retrieved the bag from the Mustang's trunk. She was already waiting in the pickup. "Is Hanson responsible for the shooting?" she asked as Rafe accelerated down the dirt road that led to the rear sections of Rancho Encantado and the Rio Grande.

"I imagine. The standard procedure is to ask questions first and shoot only as a last resort. The fact that the wetback fled back across the river would seem to indicate that the man didn't start the gunplay. Besides," he remembered, "I don't think Eddie had line watch tonight. He mentioned something about taking La Jean out to the High Lonesome."

As a matter of fact, Eddie had asked if Rafe wanted to make it a double date. But Rafe couldn't work up enough interest to even thumb through the names in his private telephone book. And he would take a vow of chastity before he'd ask Mary out again.

Manuel was waiting by the side of the road where the *hacienda*'s drive intersected it. Rafe introduced the two, and it was obvious from Manuel's flowery response that he was immediately smitten with the ivory-skinned doctor.

Like all males, Rafe thought irritably.

The pickup's headlights careened wildly over the fields, but he took his eyes off the terrain long enough to risk a glance at the enchanting nymphet beside him. Sandwiched between the two darker men, she looked like the delicious cream filling of a cookie.

She braced herself against the dashboard when the pickup took a particularly rough jolt. Cactus, mesquite, thorny chaparral and purple sage struggled for existence where the canals didn't reach. Closer to the river, cottonwoods and desert willows seemed to serve as the border's wall. They towered eerily in the sweeping flash of headlights, marking the river's course.

"More that way," Manuel instructed, pointing toward where the earth rose in a high, long embankment topped with an especially dense copse of willows.

Rafe braked the pickup at the base of the embankment. "Let's go."

The spotlight Manuel toted was their only source of light on the moonless night. Manuel pushed ahead through the thick undergrowth, and Rafe brought up the rear, keeping Mary between the two of them. Did she realize that rattlers infested the area? If she didn't, now was not the time to tell her.

He had her bag in one hand, and caught her elbow with the other, then levered her down the other side of the embankment, which was slippery with grass. They scrambled to the bottom, where shadowy branches bowed low over the water. Manuel flashed the light across the river. It was peaceful and sluggish, though Rafe knew that at floodtide it could brim its banks and sweep across the broad flat acres. A briny smell floated above the river with the low mist.

"I could have sworn, *patrón,* that *el mojado* came out of the river and fell." He pointed upstream. "Over there by that big boulder."

The river ran straight at that point and was about a hundred and forty feet wide. Most crossings were made in such areas because where the river curved, deep holes and whirlpools made it dangerous. The powerful beam moved along the far bank slowly, illuminating nothing out of the ordinary. A few large rocks, a rubber tire, driftwood.

"Perhaps the man wasn't wounded after all?" Mary suggested.

"No—there he is," Rafe said. "Downstream, about twenty-five yards. He must have crawled that far."

Manuel was already tugging off his boots to wade into the water.

"Rafe," Mary rasped, "I can't swim."

He looked askance at her. "You never learned?"

"I was too busy baby-sitting to have time for lessons at the country club!" she snapped.

He knew that fear had triggered the angry retort, and her vulnerability brought out the protective instinct in him. He repressed a laugh of self-derision. He had seen the dangerous signs of lovesickness in his other friends often enough to recognize the toehold it was gaining in him. He was crawling perilously through a mine field. With any luck he would escape unscathed when Mary left Kingdom Come.

"Take off those tennis shoes and give me the bag," was all he said. Feeling like a crane, he balanced on one foot and yanked off one boot, then the other. Mary chose to sit to remove her tennis shoes, but was just as quick as he.

Picking up her bag, he held out his hand and pulled her to her feet. "Hold on and don't let go. We're going to cross diagonally, following the current. We can wade most of the way—with the exception of maybe the last twenty or so feet."

She held his hand in a death grip, but he had to concede that she didn't give a thought to backing out.

The cool water lapped at his stocking feet. "Come on, spinster lady."

The sobriquet produced the desired effect. Her little chin tilted imperiously, and she practically marched past him into the river. But not quite.

Tugging her with him, he moved deeper into the water, feeling always for a firm bottom. He watched Manuel wading ahead of them, the floodlight lifted high over his head. Toward the river's far side the water began inching up Manuel's chest, and Rafe knew he was going to have problems with Mary because Manuel was at least half a foot taller than she. Then, too, the river bottom was muddy, causing their feet to sink a good inch or so. Mary's nails bit into the palm of his hand. Would she panic? He didn't think so.

When his foreman floundered ashore, he called out, "Manuel?"

The man turned. "*¿Sí, patrón?*"

"Catch." With a mighty effort he flung the bag overhead, and it landed not far from where Manuel stood.

"Rafe!" Mary cried out.

He looked back. The water was lapping above her breasts, and she was having trouble maintaining her balance. The current was stronger here, swirling powerfully about their torsos.

"Grab hold of my shoulders, Mary."

She did, and it was sweet agony feeling her breasts snuggling just below his shoulder blades. Her breath was warm on his neck, almost making him forget the urgency at hand for the urgency below.

Grasping handfuls of grass clumped along the sloping bank, he hauled the two of them out of the water and straggled a few feet to fall face-forward, panting. Mary lay beside him, her sweet breath fanning his face in gasping bursts. "The man," she said, and struggled to her feet to walk unsteadily toward the light that bobbled ahead, and he followed, exhausted by the exertion he had put forth.

The Mexican lay sprawled on his stomach, nude. Near him was a plastic garbage bag, securely tied— the method used to provide dry clothing, papers and food once the river was forded. He moaned unintelligibly and tried to crawl away into the brush.

"Está bien, no somos la migra," Rafe assured the cowering man.

Mary knelt beside him, and Manuel kept the light trained on the man. Her hands ran deftly, quickly over his body, and for just a fleeting second Rafe wanted to groan with jealousy. She looked up at him. "There's nothing broken, no wounds. Can you turn him over? Gently."

While she rifled through her bag, Rafe did as she had asked, easily, for the man was little and spare. Another moan of pain issued from his lips.

"Here . . . I've found the wound." It was in the right thigh, but the bleeding prevented Rafe from discerning its seriousness.

"Can you elevate the leg?" she asked him, rummaging once more in her bag. "I don't think the wound is severe. If the bullet hit the femoral artery, he'd have bled to death by now."

Rafe hunkered down and, propping the man's ankle over his knee, watched in admiration as Mary worked with an economy of motion. She applied sustained pressure just above the wound for a few moments. "The bullet?" he asked.

"The bullet must be still lodged inside." She dabbed a cotton tuft soaked in alcohol around the edges of the wound. "What was it?"

"Most likely a thirty-eight. Will he need surgery?"

"No. He's lucky. There doesn't seem to be any neurovascular injury, and as long as the bullet hasn't destroyed the bone, we can leave it in. The bleeding will cleanse the area internally." Carefully she laid folded layers of gauze compress over the area. "I'm applying a pressure dressing to control the bleeding."

The man winced as she firmly bandaged his leg to hold the dressing in place. She said, "Tell him that he must watch for swelling. He should keep the leg elevated, with ice on it, if possible. He isn't to remove the bandage for three or four days. If blood oozes into the bandage, tell him to cover it with another layer of bandaging material."

Rafe made the translation, and the man said something in reply. "He's says that he remained very still on this side of the bank for a long time before he tried to crawl away because he was afraid the Border Patrol would return to take potshots. He has a cousin in a pueblo not too far from here—maybe a couple of miles. If Manuel supports him, can he walk to the village?"

"I don't think there'll be any problem." She put the dressings back into her bag, and Rafe could see the weariness in her small oval face. "But he should stay off the injured leg as much as possible for the next few weeks or so."

She rose and Manuel helped the Mexican to his feet, bracing the man's arm across his shoulders. *"Gracias, muchas gracias,"* the Mexican told Mary.

Rafe wrapped an arm about her waist, and they watched Manuel, supporting the Mexican, start off, taking the floodlight with him. In the darkness Rafe turned to face her. That sweet face, the terribly vulnerable mouth. He was staggered by her nearness and how badly he wanted to make love to her at that moment to celebrate the triumph over the forces of evil.

Hell, he just wanted to make love to her. It was a raw hunger.

He would have lost interest in any other woman by now. Perhaps in watching her tend the wounded man he had seen her as more than just a female to enjoy for enjoyment's sake alone. Hell, he was getting positively psychotic, analyzing his feelings like a . . . a man in love.

"You ready to ford the river again, honey?" he asked, wanting to hear his own voice again, to establish some normalcy in his idiotic, rambling mind.

She shuddered in his arms and laid her head against his chest. So fine! Those breasts snuggling against him. So fine! Her hair smelled faintly of gardenias, driving him crazy with wanting. He had the intense urge to lose his fingers in her hair—and everywhere.

Her eyes looked apprehensively at the moonlit river that was deceptively quiet and sluggish. "The next position I accept, Rafe, is going to be in the middle of a desert without even a rivulet running through it."

The next position. He wasn't ready to let her go yet, at least not in the next few months. After that, well, there was always another woman to be wooed and loved. Still, the thought of another man partaking of the delights of this woman was enough to make him want to beat the sneaking weasel to a pulp.

"Time to start back," he said gruffly.

They followed the same procedure—him toting the bag, with Mary clinging to his shoulders from behind. It seemed a long way—just to the river's middle, then to the far bank, where they could retrieve their shoes, and at last to the truck. They both sat inside, regaining their breath. Finally he started the engine and picked up the track of the road. "Let's get you home and out of those wet clothes."

She looked up at him with eyes that sparkled with devilment in the dark. "Together, Rafe? I think I can manage to undress by myself, thank you, sir."

Her laughter was low and lilting, and he liked that very much. Enough to want to tease her into laughing more, just so he could hear her. But there was something more pressing on his mind right now.

"You're not even going to invite me in for a cup of coffee to reward me for rescuing you from drowning?" he asked her, not really caring what her reply was. Somehow he was going to make love to her.

"I was not drowning!"

"But I'm drowning, Mary, honey. I'm drowning in my need for you." A streak of flame was spreading through him with aggravating intensity.

He parked the truck before the adobe and caught her to him before she could escape. Her hair, damply curling, fanned out over his arm. "Oh, Mary, let me make love to you. Let me touch you everywhere." He smothered that slender, pale neck with kisses that were as smooth as a dragon's breath. He was in a rash of impatience to have her. "You have to want me as badly as I do you."

"No, not quite," she answered.

But her lips parting softly for his insistent mouth said otherwise. His hand curved about her breast, and the wet nipple thrust impudently against his palm. He rubbed it, saying, "Don't you like this?"

Her hands were cupping his face, her lips, warm and sweet, playing excitedly over his skin. "Ahh, Rafe, why do you do this to me? After fifteen minutes with you, my stomach is gnawing itself inside out and I have to eat a package of antacids."

Instantly he felt like a louse. She was so trusting. He stroked her hair, rubbing the silky damp strands between his fingers with sensuous delight. "I'm sorry, Mary. But I did warn you, honey. All's fair in love." He purposely ended the cliché at that point. "Next time . . ."

She slid from his grasp with another little laugh. At

that moment he was puzzled as to why her laughter appealed to him so much. But she was back, at least—the spirited, vivacious, fey woman who taunted him so.

"Next time?" she asked pertly. "What makes you think there will be a next time?"

He was through being the world's biggest fool. Fuming, he walked her to the door, his hands thrust in his jeans pockets to keep them from having their way with Dr. Mary Margulies.

At the door she turned and looked up at him sweetly. "Do I get a good-night kiss?"

When the church mission board next requested a doctor, it was going to specify sex: male. He caught her shoulders and kissed her gently on the forehead. There, that ought to put her in her place. But when he saw the forlorn little pout on her lips, he made up for his crassness by kissing her twice more on the mouth, quickly, roughly. Then, leaving her standing at the door, he strode to the pickup, feeling elated at having won the battle of the sexes.

Chapter 8

LA JEAN POKED HER HEAD INSIDE MARY'S OFFICE. "Hermalinda is here."

Mary closed her eyes and rubbed her temples, then said, "Put her in the first waiting room—and keep a watch on the street."

She looked down at the ledger she had been going over. Only nineteen patients that month. Six on Medicare; one, an old wino she hadn't charged; and several, with complaints of minor ailments, whom she had either met at Eddie's party or who had been sent over by Father John.

Naturally in a town of such small population she hadn't counted on servicing a stadium-size crowd every month. But twenty patients was not even half the capacity on which she had based the clinic's monthly budget. She could only be thankful that the church and community were partially subsidizing the clinic.

Recalling the patient she had waiting, she rose to her feet—reluctantly. True, Hermalinda Hernández was willing to pay. But at what cost to Mary's own career if she were caught treating the young woman?

The woman sat on the examining table, fully clothed. Her face wore that soft expression associated with mothers-to-be, and her stubby, reddened fingers were interlocked over her burgeoning abdomen in a maternal, protective gesture. She looked almost beautiful. Well, almost attractive. "*Buenos días, soltera.*"

Mary repressed a smile and said sternly, "I heard that *la migra* arrested and deported you."

"*Sí.* But I am back, as you can see." Her triumphant smile edged into one of determination. "My child will be born a citizen of the United States."

Mary began taking her blood pressure. "I've told you, Hermalinda, I can't deliver your baby."

The girl shrugged her shoulders and smiled placidly. "*Que será, será.*"

Mary knew that phrase well enough, and she knew that Hermalinda was counting on more than whatever would be, would be. Hermalinda was counting on Mary to accede at the last moment. But the young Mexican girl didn't realize that Dr. Mary Margulies had a will and determination just as strong as her own. "I hate to destroy your deep faith in humanity, Hermalinda, but I can't and won't jeopardize my career to deliver your baby."

She noted the girl's blood pressure, then had her

stand on the scales. "Holy Moses, Hermalinda! Did you eat your way through a tortilla factory? You've gained five pounds!"

Hermalinda giggled, displaying her widely spaced front teeth. "Perhaps I carry *dos bebés—gemelos*."

Mary's expression darkened. "Let's hope not. You're far too narrow in the pelvis to deliver twins. Not, at least, without the assistance of a doctor."

"But I have a doctor," the girl said, unconcerned at the possibility. "You."

"Only for the next few months," Mary replied firmly, staunchly, but far from coolly. "And observing your progress does not include bringing your child into the world. Do you understand me?"

That silly grin again. A tolerant assurance that ultimately she would have her way.

"Look, Hermalinda, if *la migra* walks into the clinic this very moment, you'll go back to El Paso's detention center."

"Bah!" Hermalinda snapped her fingers disdainfully. "I check. *La migra* is south of here on patrol."

"Don't underestimate the Border Patrol in this section, Hermalinda. Chief Hanson can be very shrewd and very . . . difficult."

Hermalinda slipped her worn huaraches back on her splayed feet. "This Hanson, he is a very small man inside, I think."

Mary was impressed by the Indian girl's insight. Also, she was worried about Hermalinda, but the young girl was street-wise and undoubtedly knew how to handle Hanson and his kind better than most.

Curiosity overcame Mary. "What does your husband say about you risking your freedom, even your life, to cross the border? You know, you're risking the life of your child—his child, too."

A derisive hoot. "Husband, *soltera?* With fifteen children to feed, my parents, they were very poor. They sell me to a bordello. I was fourteen. I learn English from the customers there. Last month I buy my freedom from the bordello. This *bebé*"—her hand caressed her stomach—"I don't know who its father is. I do know, *soltera,* that the *bebé* will get a better chance than me. The *bebé* will be a U.S. citizen."

Mary sighed. "Watch out for *la migra,*" she told the departing girl.

It was by now afternoon. Friday afternoon. And no word from Rafe for an entire week. So, it was to be the old one-upsmanship game.

Why couldn't a man and a woman just be friends? Why couldn't kissing just be enough? Why did a man have to score with every woman he knew? Perhaps she *was* naive. A naive thirty-five-year-old virgin. A naive thirty-five-year-old spinster.

Loathsome labels.

Mary's fingers fumbled with her panty hose in her impatience to smooth them over her legs. She glanced at the clock on her nightstand. Three-thirty-eight. Still plenty of time before the Greyhound bus was due to stop at Vicente's *tienda*.

It had been more than three months since she had seen Billy. On her move to Kingdom Come, she had stopped off to visit him in Midland, where he was working in the Permian Basin oil patch. Those three months were the longest interval she had gone without seeing him since she had begun her tour of duty for the NHSC. Before that, during those tough years of making it through college and med school, she had always managed to make a home for him and Amy with her.

There had been arguments, of course, when one of the two had been determined to question her authority—and she had often been frightened sick that Amy or Bill would actually flout her ruling of the moment and leave. They didn't understand, at their tender ages, that they were a family, no matter what the conditions. They were all the family that any of them had.

And there had been the difficult times when money just wouldn't stretch enough to cover both their lunches and hers. She went without. Or the times when they took her for granted . . . the time when Amy used the lunch money frivolously on expensive makeup. For Mary, there had been no makeup during those teenage years.

But there had also been the close, warm times. The time Billy had made Mary a birthday cake that had tasted suspiciously like biscuit mix. Mary had laughed. And she had cried. She had never before had a birthday party.

The telephone interrupted Mary's reverie. Hurriedly she zipped up her halter-top dress splashed with white dots on black seersucker and grabbed for the receiver. "Hello," she said tersely, cradling the receiver in the hollow of her shoulder while she slid into black-and-white spectator pumps.

"Mary?" It was Rafe.

Why was he invading her life again? "Yes?"

"I don't feel so well." His voice was raspy. "Can you come over and see what's wrong?"

"What's wrong is probably no more than a hangover," she said crisply.

"No . . . honestly, Mary . . . I feel like hell. Must be the flu or something."

She glanced at the clock. Billy would be arriving in less than twenty minutes. "Call Josefita. I'm sure she'll have some home remedy for your ailment."

"But she can't stroke my forehead with loving care like you can."

That sounded more like the old Rafe. "Sorry. My brother Billy is arriving on the four-o'clock bus, and I have to meet him."

"You owe me a consultation for the flat I changed." Then he added, "Please."

It wasn't like Rafe to beg. He was normally as haughty as a *hidalgo*. And he did sound lousy. "All right," she conceded with a sigh. "Let me pick up Billy, and I'll swing by on my way back."

On her way out the door she grabbed her medical bag. She was no doubt a fool, falling for such an old ploy as Rafe was using, but she'd have Billy with her, which would forestall any of Rafe's amorous advances.

The streamlined silver bus rolled to a halt before Vicente's just as she parked the Mustang. Billy swung out, and her silly heart was pushing at her throat. What had happened to the little boy with the runny nose and the inevitable pet cricket in his shirt pocket? Coming toward her with long, eager strides was a tall, lanky young man with tousled reddish-brown hair and a boyish smile that disengaged her heart's machinery.

"Sis!" He dropped the duffel bag and caught her up against him and swung her in a circle.

At last he set her down, and the pedestrians ambling by turned curious heads and smiled broadly, caught up in the affectionate greeting of the two people. "Billy." It was all she could manage for a moment. "Stand back, let me look at you. My, my, just look at you." Her fingertips poked at his upper lip. "And a real mustache, no less. No peach fuzz this time."

He wore a bashful grin that said he was as pleased as punch with himself. He might as well have rubbed the toe of his scuffed boot in a circle. "Well, I'm a working man now, sis."

"So you are. But not for the Labor Day weekend. It's going to be strictly relaxation and fun. Get your bag, and we'll go home."

But as she drove back to Rancho Encantado she worried what fun she could offer a healthy young man like him. How was she going to entertain him? And she still had to stop off at Rafe's. Not much of a way to start a holiday weekend.

Billy chattered on about his work and his friends on the oil-rig crews until she drove across the stone bridge. "Holy Moses, sis. Is that where you live?"

He was looking at the palatial *hacienda* that dominated the landscape. "No." She hated to crush his illusions. "There." She pointed at the garish pink-and-turquoise adobe box.

"Oh."

"But we're going to visit the *hacienda* right now. I have to call on a patient—a friend—who owns the place."

"Allll right!"

A barefoot Rafe greeted them at the door. He was dressed in jeans but was shirtless. His butter-yellow curls were matted, and his normally bronzed face was pasty. "Mary, honey," he groaned, "I feel like horse manure."

Beside her, Billy's eyes narrowed at the endearment that Rafe had used. "Billy, this is Rafe Anaya. Rafe, my brother Billy Margulies." Both nodded, Billy grudgingly, Rafe weakly. "Let me check you over," she told Rafe in a professional tone.

Rafe led them inside and slumped onto the long leather couch. Newspapers, a pair of worn boots and empty glasses were strewn about the room. "Sorry about the mess," he mumbled with a vague sweep of his hand. "Carmelita only comes twice a week to clean."

So, no wonder he didn't need a wife. He had Carmelita to clean and Christina and doubtless an army of other willing women to provide him with nightly pleasures. Briskly she opened her bag and began to examine him. He rested his head passively against the sofa's high back, his thick lashes looking like black sickles against the pale skin of his high cheekbones.

She took out her stethoscope, holding it against the hard expanse of his chest. His lids snapped open. "The thing's as cold as a Laplander's nose!" he complained.

"Hush," she said, and proceded to take his temperature, wishing he would close his eyes again. The way his gaze perused her face made her uncomfortable. "One-oh-one," she pronounced.

Disinterested, Billy, hands thrust in his jeans, turned away to look out the wall of glass that gave a view of the distant mountains. "Wow!" she heard him say. She looked around to see her brother ogling the immense pool outside. Never having been at the *hacienda* during the day, she had not noticed the swimming pool, which was partially camouflaged by a stand of bamboo and some kind of exotic flowering shrubbery.

"You could float the Texas Navy in that tank!" Billy said.

"Go float your body, if you want," Rafe offered in what was meant to be a genial tone but was punctuated with a raspy cough. "Got several extra pairs of swim trunks in the *cabaña*."

"Allll right!"

"Billy," she checked, but he was already out the sliding glass door, heading down the flagstone walk to the adobe *cabaña* that looked only slightly smaller than the *caporal*'s quarters in which she lived.

Reluctantly she turned her attention back to Rafe and effeciently pressed the wooden blade against his tongue, taking almost fiendish delight in his discomforted, "Agggh. Is that necessary, honey?"

"Yes." She caught his beard-shadowed jaw and turned his head to one side to examine his ears.

"Well?" he asked. "Am I dying of advanced leprosy?"

At last, putting away the otoscope, she said, "Common cold."

"Common cold?" he groaned. "But I feel so uncommonly terrible. It has to be much worse."

"Well," she conceded, "you do have a minor virus. I prescribe a couple of days in bed, aspirin every four hours and plenty of liquids. I'll pick up a sample bottle of antihistamine at the clinic for you."

She rose, closed her bag and went to the door to call Billy. He was in the act of executing a swan dive that collapsed ignominiously into a belly-buster. "Let him swim," Rafe grunted from the couch. "You can pick him up when you return."

On the way to the clinic she told herself that Billy was having a good time and that that was what she wanted for him. But she hated being beholden to Rafe. With it being Friday, La Jean had already left for the long weekend, and Mary let herself in, collected the medicine and started back to Rancho

Encantado. On the way she stopped at Vicente's for a couple of large cans of frozen orange juice. Rafe obviously didn't feel up to taking care of himself.

When she let herself in the *hacienda* Billy was still flapping as joyously as a seal in the water. She prepared a pitcher of orange juice and, setting a glass of it along with the antihistamine and aspirin on a hand-painted tray she located, went in search of Rafe. In the fourth bedroom, a very masculine room done in gold and brown, she found him sprawled diagonally on a large bed, facedown. Evening's faint sunlight patinaed his flesh where it stretched tautly across his shoulders.

When she set the tray on the nightstand Rafe rolled to his back and propped himself on his elbows. With one hand she held out the glass of orange juice and in her other palm two aspirin. "You're not going to let me off, are you?" he asked, glowering at her.

"No. Now, take the aspirin and you'll be over this within forty-eight hours."

In one gulp he swallowed the aspirin and downed the orange juice. "Satisfied, Dr. Margulies?" he growled irritably.

She took the empty glass and set it on the tray, then smiled sweetly. "You could have had Josefita, but you wanted me."

"I still do," he said huskily, and caught her wrist before she could step away from the bed. "Ahhh, Mary, stay the weekend with me and look after your patient."

Her mouth opened in protest, and he said, "Billy would enjoy himself here."

That she had to acknowledge. She didn't even own a television set. Still, she was reluctant to stay at his house, to expose herself to the opportunity of getting to know him more intimately.

About her wrist his hand was feverish, and that professional consideration decided her. "All right."

The drooping ends of his mustache twitched with his effort at a grin. It was followed by a victorious grunt as he rolled back onto his stomach and flaked out.

The kid in a floppy bamboo hat, hardly more than ten or so, was standing in the shallow ditch at the side of the dirt road. Muddy water washed about his ankles. In his hand he held what looked like a can of cola. He waved and smiled one of those toothy grins as the first few soldiers straggled by. A sergeant with the Fifth Infantry tossed the Vietnamese urchin a half-eaten candy bar and plodded on past.

But as Rafe watched from his position on the second tank in formation, the kid made no effort to catch the candy bar. Unusual. All kids—everyone— was hungry those days. Then, before his suspicions could coalesce, the kid was hurling the cola can at the first tank. Rafe tried to open his mouth to shout a warning. He tried. And tried. But the tank exploded in a burst of orange flame.

The kid took off running—just as a private toward

the front of the line swung his automatic around. The .30-caliber bullets kicked up the dust at the boy's feet, then . . .

"No!" Rafe shouted, and bolted upright in his bed. Sweat was pouring off him.

Almost immediately Mary stumbled into the room, her golden robe glimmering in the slivers of moonlight. "Rafe . . . are you all right?"

Sometimes, even when he was awake, he could still see one of the kid's thongs, childishly small, as it hurtled through the air. In his more rational moments he knew that that tiny thong was a part of the reason why he never wanted to fight again. It was a resolution he had not broken, not once since returning to the States, despite all the brawling bars he had drunk his way through.

He wiped the sweat from his brow with the back of his forearm. "Yeah. Just a bad dream."

She didn't ask him to tell her about it—when he hated talking about it; she didn't tell him that it was just a dream and to go on back to sleep—when the dream would only invade his sleep again. Rather she gently touched his shoulder and said in that softly modulated voice of hers, "I'll fix some green tea."

Incredibly, she understood him.

He knew then, as he watched the golden glimmer leave his bedroom, that when she left Kingdom Come he wasn't going to be quite the free-spirited bachelor of old. Two days with her caring for him, tending him, had left him wanting her more than ever. She reminded him in some ways of his grandmother, who had nursed him through the chickenpox and the measles with the same brisk—but loving—efficiency. Of course, Mary had made it quite plain that she wasn't ready to fall in love with anyone.

But he already had.

If there were any woman he would want to settle down with, it would be Mary. But his whole life had been one of moving. As a child he had been shuttled from one diplomatic post to another, the different cities nothing but a blur; later, with the Special Forces, he had been constantly relocating with Army Intelligence headquarters, the only home phone he had. He didn't think it was possible for a man like him to settle down. Not forever, with one woman.

Without bothering to pull on any briefs, he slid into his jeans and followed her out into the kitchen. Beneath the bright fluorescent lights she was measuring out the tea, brisk, practical, Dr. Margulies. He leaned against the counter, arms folded, bare feet crossed, and watched her. He liked her fluid movements. He liked the way a wisp of red-brown hair coiled about the tender white flesh of her neck. Under the intensity of his gaze her movements faltered, but she visibly regrouped herself and, setting down the package of tea, said in her professional voice, "I believe you're over the virus. Here, let me feel your—"

He caught her fingers as she reached out to touch his forehead and drew her against him. "I'm hot, Mary. But the fever's because of you."

"Rafe, no." She stiffened within the circle of his arms.

"Good grief, Mary, you're not some kind of saint. You're not St. Mary—you're flesh and blood. Alive, breathing, made for loving."

And despite his intentions not to make love to her, he *was* loving her—whispering his adoration of her against that delicate ear, stroking her neck, fastening his lips on hers as if he'd never let her go. Her soft little mews of surrender were crashing against that primitive part of him like tidal waves.

"The teakettle's whistling."

The harsh male voice broke the two of them apart. With Mary thrust behind him, Rafe whirled, still trying to catch his breath, and saw Billy standing in the doorway. He wore pajama bottoms that Rafe had never used. Below the rumpled hair the boy's—young man's—face wore a resentful, belligerent look.

Rafe drew on all his old training in outwaiting and outwitting, in calm but swift deliberation. "Why, so it is, Billy. Thanks." He turned his back on the boy, knowing full well that Billy wanted nothing better than to smash a right into him. He crossed the kitchen and removed the piping teakettle from the stove. "Mary? Want a cup?"

She was quick, as he had come to know she would be. "Yes. With a teaspoon of sugar, Rafe. Billy, how about you?"

Billy's narrowed eyes slid to his sister. Uncertainty showed in his face. "No."

Only when he whirled from the doorway and retreated to his bedroom did Mary allow the agitation to show in her lovely face. "Oh, Rafe, he must think the worst!"

"And what is the worst, Mary?" He handed her a cup. "That you're a woman with a woman's needs?"

"You don't understand." Her eyes pleaded. "I'm like his mother."

"And like all sons, he's going through the jealousy period." He cupped her cheek with one hand. "Mary, only when he sees you outside the mother role will he be fully released to become his own man."

"But I wanted this weekend with him to go so well, Rafe!"

"I'll take care of it, honey." He sighed, wondering why he was entangling himself deeper with Mary and her life. It was one of his policies never to commit himself beyond the next evening of entertainment.

He was still weak, too weak to work at seducing this fascinating woman, and, setting down his cup, he kissed her chastely on the forehead and returned to bed. The next day was going to be a strenuous one.

Rafe tugged the Stetson lower over his brow to block the brilliant morning sun. He still felt as weak as a cold car battery. He glanced over at Billy, who was handling the lop-eared roan fairly well, considering that it was his first time astride. Of course the kid would never admit to being nervous.

"Esmeralda's Manuel's mount," Rafe said. "He uses her to check the sections that are tough to reach by truck."

Billy said nothing—half, Rafe guessed, out of resentment left over from the night before and half out of preoccupation with controlling the mare.

Rafe continued in the same easy vein. "Manuel usually handles pump problems, but he's off to visit his mother-in-law. Glad you know something about 'em." He flicked the boy a wry grin. "Even if it is a water pump instead of an oil pump."

Silence. So much for that attempt at establishing rapport.

Dust churned up by a tractor billowed ahead, and Rafe reined his mount around the field. A couple of miles farther west they reached the gate for canal number six. The pump had been down for five days, but the field it irrigated was fallow, so there was no rush to repair it.

But Billy wouldn't know that. Or that Rafe rarely handled the maintenance problems anymore. Keeping up with the paperwork of Rancho Encantado took enough time as it was.

He removed the saddle kit full of tools and went to work. After only a few minutes it became evident that Billy did know his stuff, and the repair job went more quickly than it would have if Rafe had done it alone. He halted once to shrug out of his shirt, damp with perspiration, and Billy followed suit. The source of the problem was a loose belt. Rafe thought they must look like two efficient surgeons operating on a delicate patient, with Billy passing him the necessary tool, before he even had to ask for it.

On the ride back Rafe contained his impatience. He

knew that the subject would have to be broached now or never. And by Billy. Still, Rafe talked lightly of the ranch and its problems. "Even here—in the middle of nowhere—you have to keep up with modern technology. See that tractor over there?" He tipped his head in the direction of the dust whorl. "It's no ordinary piece of machinery. Uses a laser beam to even out the ground to the millimeter."

That caught Billy's attention real fast. "No kidding!"

"For sure." He let it lapse at that and rode along again in silence—hoping.

At last, "You sweet on my sister?" Billy asked.

"I hanker after her, all right."

More silence.

"You gonna marry her?"

"Don't think either of us is ready to marry. How about you? Found anyone you ready to settle down with?"

"Naww. Gotta get the kinks out of my legs first."

Rafe breathed a little easier. "Guess it just takes some of us longer than others."

"Yeah. 'Specially men. Got me this little woman over in Midland what's just itching to tie the knot."

"Don't think your sister is."

"Yeah, well . . . can't see as how I blame her at all. She's been a mother all her life as it is. Sorta glad to see her enjoying herself without getting all tied down."

"You got a point there, son."

Chapter 9

RATHER THAN GO HOME WHEN THE CLINIC CLOSED AND while away another long Friday evening alone, Mary decided to make a side trip through the *barrio* again. Somehow before her term was up she meant to convince the people of the valley that she was a capable, qualified doctor.

She had to wonder why their approval would mean so much to her when she wasn't going to be here much longer. She must be losing her mind—over Rafe.

Luck was with her, for Mrs. Ruiz was out in the yard hanging freshly washed clothes on the hemp line. Quickly, before the woman could run and hide in her house, Mary got out of the car and crossed to her. "Hello, Mrs. Ruiz. How is the baby doing?"

Ofelia rubbed her damp hands down the front of

her dress and hunched her bony shoulders in an indifferent shrug. "Pedro is over there. He is fine."

"Over there" meant on a blanket spread beneath the meager shade of the mesquite tree that also served as one post for the clothesline. Conscious of the mother's guarded eyes on her, Mary walked over to kneel before the infant. He was on his back, his little fists sparring like a boxer's at some imaginary punching bag. His black eyes, once a jaundiced cast, were bird-bright.

"The medicine helped!" Mary exclaimed, exuberant at her first success in the *barrio*.

The woman took a wooden clothespin from her mouth and anchored a wash-yellowed T-shirt to the line. "Pedro didn't take the medicine."

Mary blinked. Her brain blinked.

"*La curandera* healed Pedro."

Mary shot to her feet and crossed over to the woman. "Why, Mrs. Ruiz?" She tried to keep the hurt out of her voice. She certainly wasn't behaving professionally, but she had been pushed too far. "Why didn't you even give me a chance?"

The woman had the good grace to duck her head. "*Soltera*, you will leave one day. But *la curandera,* she will be here always. After her, her daughter Carmelita will become *la curandera.*" The woman raised her head to meet Mary's dumbfounded gaze. "And *la curandera* will never again treat any of us who seek your help."

"I see." She saw all too clearly. The whole valley seemed to be in conspiracy against her.

She turned and marched to her car. She wanted only to drive it as far as she could from Kingdom Come. But she couldn't. She was committed by contract to stay the term. Less than four months to go, she mentally tallied on the drive back home.

Both cars were parked in front of the *hacienda's* garage, and she was sorely tempted to drive on up to the house. She badly needed to share her rotten day with someone. She badly needed Rafe to kiss her into a delirium and tell her everything would be all right. She even got as far as the turnoff to the *hacienda*'s driveway before she put a halt to her folly. What if he had a guest? Christina Andersson? Or Josefita's lovely sloe-eyed daughter, Carmelita?

Embarrassed at how close she had come to making a fool of herself, she turned the car and retraced the road to her adobe. Last weekend at Rafe's had been a mistake. Oh, Billy had gone away happy. He had enjoyed himself immensely, and he and Rafe had talked like old war buddies on the way to meet the bus. And that was just the problem—she had caught another glimpse of Rafe that made him just that much more likable. And that was something she didn't like.

Did he regret embroiling himself in her family affairs? Was that why he had made no effort to see her? Perhaps it was just as well—for both their sakes.

After a vegetarian dinner she rewarded herself for adhering to her Spartan diet with a long, leisurely bath. She disrobed, hanging her clothes carefully. Never having had the privacy of her own bedroom and closet as a child, she was compunctiously neat with her clothes. And with everything else. Everything had its place.

In the tarnished mirror of the terra-cotta-tiled bathroom she studied her reflection critically.

"Mirror, mirror, on the wall . . .

"Not so bad for a middle-aged spinster," she wryly told the pot of English ivy. "Small breasts, but firm and high. No varicose veins or stretch marks, or even orange-peel dimpled skin."

Hands on her hips, she pirouetted to glimpse her derriere. "Well . . . perhaps that part of your anatomy could be a trifle less voluptuous, Mary Margulies. More like those nearly curveless flanks of Christina Andersson."

She soaked in the warm, bubbly bathwater, her head resting on the tub's edge, and thought about that first day in Kingdom Come and her first bath—or her first attempt at a bath. She could feel the heat of a blush that had nothing to do with the steamy water steal over her. For Rafe to have caught her almost as nude as Goya's *Maja*—at that moment she couldn't think of anything worse.

Except maybe deluding herself into thinking that a relationship with Rafe could be a safe, platonic one. He was a menace to all her hopes and plans.

The soft lapping of the water about her breasts, which protuded from the bubble bath like miniature coral islands, recalled Rafe's hungry caresses there. The image of him, his smoldering eyes lustily heavy-lidded, scored the backs of her lids. The memory of his hands, hard and hot, frenziedly questing over her body, stirred up conflicting feelings of reticence and desire.

Abruptly she sat up and began scrubbing vigorously, wishing there were some way she could scrub away the memory of his warm laughter, his delicious way with words, his attentive way of listening. She knew she loved him. But there was no future in that love. He wanted no emotional involvement, and for her there could be nothing less. Because caring was all she knew how to do.

On Saturday she puttered about the house barefoot and in shorts, cleaning, dusting and washing clothes. The cooler hummed away, despite the fact it was September. Intense color-killing sunlight splayed on the unglazed mud tiles. It promised to be a slow day, and a little after noon she drove into Kingdom Come to Vicente's, hoping a letter from Amy or Billy would enliven her day a little.

On the way back to the adobe she rifled through the mail she had received. The light bill, some mail-order magazines and—Eureka!—a note from Amy. She slit the envelope open with excited fingers and began reading the two-page letter. A quarter of an hour later she put it down on the kitchen table with a small, fervent sigh of thanksgiving. Amy was apparently doing well with her college courses and liked her roommate.

She spent the rest of the afternoon writing letters to Amy and Billy. Each ended with her love and included a check. A college student always needed the money. And Billy . . . Obviously he no longer needed her financial support; she supposed the gesture was just a result of the maternal instinct she had developed over the years of watching over her brothers and sisters.

When she had finished with her letters she felt at loose ends. She wasn't hungry enough to cook anything, and she paced about the small adobe. She wouldn't let herself glance out the window at the *hacienda* down the road. At the telephone's shrill ring she jerked around and stared at it as if it were a scorpion on the wall.

Tentatively she picked up the receiver. "Hello?" Her voice sounded so breathless that she didn't recognize it as belonging to herself.

"Mary?"

"Oh. Hi, Beau."

If he noticed her lack of enthusiasm he didn't indicate it in any way. "You been jogging or something? You sound out of breath."

"No, I was at the back of the house."

"I was afraid I wouldn't catch you at home this evening. I've got two tennis rackets. How about playing tomorrow afternoon at Christina's? She's offered me the use of her courts anytime I want them."

That meant she was offering Beau—in exchange for Rafe. "I don't know how to play tennis, Beau."

"Great! I'll teach you. What do you say?"

She should take him up on his offer. Who wanted to sit around alone on a gorgeous Sunday afternoon? "All right, Beau."

"Fine. Pick you up at one o'clock after church."

"Great. I'd like that."

Rafe didn't. Especially when Mary and Beau met as they entered the chapel Sunday morning and by mutual consent sat together. Rafe glared at Beau all through Mass. Vicente, who was with Rafe, intercepted the evil eye that Rafe cast at his opponent. The shark was fighting hard to escape, Vicente thought, but he would put his *dinero* with the pretty little fisherwoman—except she didn't seem to be that interested in reeling in the catch.

Dressed in a vanilla-colored nubby textured suit, Mary sat with her hands folded demurely in her lap. Once, when Beau laid his arm behind her on the back of the pew, she thought Rafe was going to grab Vicente's rosary and strangle Beau.

From the pulpit Father John looked down on this interplay with a benign smile and continued his sermon on the blessings of marriage.

Christina's house by daylight was even more imposing than it had seemed the night of the party. The two-story-white-brick house angled off in what seemed a dozen different wings, and massive pillars supported a veranda that ran the length of the front. Its Southern-plantation architecture looked completely out of place in the desert landscape.

"Do people really live here?" she asked.

Beau, who looked great in white tennis shorts and a knit shirt, smiled at Mary's naiveté. She was utterly enchanting—especially in her pink shorts that displayed her perfectly shaped legs. "Only when it snows in New Hampshire."

The double tennis courts were at the rear of the house, along with riding stables and an Olympic-size pool set in an artificial tropical landscape. Christina was nowhere to be seen. No doubt she was engaged in another sort of game with Rafe.

Beau proceeded to teach Mary the rules of tennis, giving plenty of attention to the strokes, which permitted him to touch Mary often. After more than an hour she was able to return the ball—but into the court next to theirs. After the third such lob she stopped, hands on hips, and glared at Beau, who was having his own difficulty concentrating on the game when the delightful anatomy on the other side of the net was so distracting.

"I fail to see the pleasure in this game," she said, and blew at the fat curl that wafted down over her nose. Perspiration adhered her tank top to her upper torso, emphasizing her heaving breasts. "It's frustrating!"

"But, Mary, dear," Christina said, choosing that moment to make her appearance in a smashing white maillot swimsuit, "tennis is so marvelous for the figure."

Mary watched the other woman prop her suntanned willowy frame against the net's post and conceded that sheer will maintained such a splendid figure. "Then you must play often," she said, trying to be a polite guest.

"No. I detest getting sweaty, dear." She turned her attention away from Mary. "When you two finish, Beau, you must join us for a swim to cool off." From behind the sleek swath of silver-white hair she tossed a sidelong glance at Mary. "I've invited Rafe and a few others."

Mary knew then that she was tired of tennis—and Christina Andersson. She declined the invitation.

Beau was just as happy to be alone with her. Rafe hadn't cornered the market yet. "Want to get a drink, Mary?" he asked as he drove back into town.

She really didn't, but the knowledge that Rafe was probably getting Christina all sweaty prompted her to yield to Beau's suggestion. She didn't want to go into the Oasis bar in shorts, but neither did she want to go to Beau's house, which had been his second suggestion.

The beer was cold and refreshing, and she would just bet that Christina didn't drink anything so common. In the bar's dimness she and Beau talked lightly of their respective careers, Kingdom Come's slow economy and the nuclear-waste plant going in up at Carlsbad. Beau was attentive, especially to her sweat-sheened cleavage.

Rafe would have been impossible at this point, she knew.

Dusk was hazing the mountains by the time Beau walked her to her door and put his arm about her waist. "Mary, I can't tell you how much I enjoy being with you."

She didn't want him to tell her how much he enjoyed being with her because she knew it was the prelude to a kiss, which she certainly was not ready to bestow. "Thank you for the fun afternoon, Beau."

But he wasn't ready to let her go. He pulled her close to him. "How about a good-night kiss, Mary?" he murmured against her temple.

Gingerly she extricated herself from the hands that were beginning to roam. "I think not."

"Why not?"

"Why, because it's not sanitary, Beau," she said with a straight face. "You never know what germ you'll pick up."

Confusion clouded his handsome face. "Oh. All right." He didn't press the issue but released her, unsure of her seriousness. Rafe would have been nibbling at her neck, oblivious of her sly dismissal.

No sooner had she gotten inside and changed out of her clothes than there was a knock at the door. Still in her slip and panty hose, she went into the living room. "Who is it?" she called.

"Rafe," a masculine voice growled. "It didn't take Brewster long to see you to the door," he said in a tone that couldn't conceal his male satisfaction.

Rafe must have been watching and waiting from his house. She leaned back against the door, eyes closed and a reckless smile playing at the ends of her lips. "Ahhh, but Beau can do in a minute what it takes some men hours to do," she called back.

"Damned, Mary, if you don't deserve a beating. Let me in."

"I can't. I'm not fully dressed."

"Are you ever? Go put something on while I make some green tea. I brought my own package."

She sprinted to her bedroom and wrapped the

satiny robe about her. It was getting more use in a couple of months than it had seen in years. In the kitchen she could hear Rafe making himself at home, and she took the time to let down her hair, fluffing it into a rowdy mass of curls about her shoulders, and place a faint dab of perfume at the pulse point of her neck and on the insides of her elbows.

Perhaps what she was doing was futile, but she so desperately wanted him to respond to her on more than just a physical level—on an emotional level. The same feelings she had given and received from her brothers and sisters—they were still necessary to her. Feelings of warmth and caring—if only he would admit to those feelings.

At the kitchen door she stood and let her eyes soak in the man who had so changed her life. His back was to her as he poured the tea. The tiled counter on both sides of him was already a mess of discarded spoons, a sugar bowl, two cups, a wadded paper towel, a tea strainer and the open package of green tea.

But her gaze swept over the mess without a flicker of an annoyed eyelash, to roam over the man. His boots made him even taller, if that were possible. His faded jeans, snugly molding his narrow hips, looked as if he had worn them so much that if he stepped out of them they would retain their shape.

He turned to set the cups on the table, and a devilish smile creased his face. Oh, Lord, but he was gorgeous. "Mary, honey, my fingers are just itching to romp through your hair."

She managed to cast him a stern look and took a

seat at the table, careful to keep the robe's folds in place. "You wanted to talk to me?"

He chugged down the hot tea like it was whiskey meant to fortify him. Then he rose, strode to the counter and returned with a bottle. "This is for you."

She took the bottle and read the label. Antacids.

"This is to settle your stomach," he was saying, "because you and I are going to start dating again."

She set the bottle down, trying to repress the mirth that bubbled inside her. "I don't know, Rafe. I—"

"You dated Beau, you can date me."

"But with Beau I feel so safe."

"We'll double-date, then. With Eddie and La Jean."

"And Christina? Didn't you have a date with her this afternoon?"

He placed his hands on the table to either side of her. "Mary, honey, I'm not a man to be tied down. You can understand that, can't you?"

So, it was still to be his rules. But then, he was right. And she was not a woman to be tied down.

"I'll give it a try," she compromised. "Once."

He looked terribly pleased that she had accepted his proposal so easily and put no pressure on him to see only her. His hand reached out to finger a wandering curl that had tumbled behind her ear.

"Don't do that!" she said.

"Do what, Mary?" he teased.

"You know what you do to me, Rafe Anaya."

He swallowed mightily. "I can't help myself." He

rose to his feet. "But I'm leaving. And I'm leaving the green tea. For my future visits."

She trailed him to the front door, and before she could back off he turned and caught her, his arms wrapped loosely about her waist. "You've got to find some kind of granny robe to wear instead of this"— one hand released her long enough to make a helpless gesture—"this slinky thing. Or else I can't be held responsible for—"

She backed out of his reach. "Rafe!"

"For my lusty thoughts." With that he caught her to him again, kissed her on her upturned nose and left her standing in the doorway, completely bemused.

Chapter 10

HE HAD TO BE THE WORLD'S BIGGEST FOOL. MARY HAD him in the palm of her hand. He might as well be gelded. These days he couldn't find a woman who held his interest even in mere conversation, let alone anything beyond.

Except for Mary.

Dammit, that was just what the delightful little creature sitting next to him in the pickup had done. She had effectively gelded him with all her rules when he had picked her up that evening. "Just friends and fun," she had stated firmly, fists planted on those enticing hips where his hands ought to be. "Remember, no more seduction attempts," she had admonished, then proceeded to tick off other rules on her fingers.

He would have left her standing there enumerating her regulations like a schoolmarm, but he had been too absorbed with the way her nipples were gloriously outlined by the dress's thin, slinky material.

Then, before he knew it, he was acceding to her rules. Docilely, like an old bull being put to pasture. All for the privilege of sitting next to her. He had to be out of his head. If he didn't watch himself, she would become a Magnificent Obsession with him.

Frowning at his predicament, he squinted even more against the western sun, setting brillantly. Every time he began to work up a good righteous anger Mary would squeeze a little closer to him—compliments of La Jean and Eddie packed into the cab with them—and his anger would evaporate. Her thigh flanked alongside his created all sorts of disturbing images in his mind that weren't conducive to maintaining a normal blood-pressure level.

He had to stop fantasizing all the time about Mary. He wasn't getting any work done at the ranch or in his office! And the last date he had had with another woman, only a week or so after the lovable, adorable Dr. Mary Margulies had hit town, he had taken her home early because he could think of little else besides the luscious little spinster. Funny, he couldn't even remember the other woman's name now.

And he couldn't forget Mary.

"Hey, Rafe." Eddie leaned forward. "Your expression would chill a jalapeño. We've been laughing ourselves silly over China Polly—the way she sprin-

kles her laundry by spraying water from her mouth—
and you sit behind the wheel looking like you lost the
battle of the Alamo."

"Please, Eddie," Mary rebuffed with mock indigna-
tion, "I'll have no discriminatory remarks about my
date for the evening." She laid her hand consolingly
on Rafe's thigh, and his jeans seemed to shrink
instantaneously. "After all, he is paying for our
entertainment at the High Lonesome tonight."

"Only because he lost the bet about Hanson. You
should've known, ol' friend, that Hanson could down
seven bottles of mescal last night and still put a plug
through each and every empty bottle."

"The son of a—"

"Rafe!" Mary reproved, laughing with La Jean.

They were having a good time, enjoying each
other's company. And his friends liked Mary—adored
her—if their comments in their idle hours were any
indication. He adored her, too—almost enough to
make him forget his single-minded purpose: making
love to Dr. Mary Margulies.

He was feeling rather irritated and slightly sorry for
himself—and yet tremendously satisfied with himself
at the same time because Mary was there sitting next
to him. Why couldn't she be satisfied with loving him
for the short time they had together? The mere idea of
settling down sent shivers up his spine, despite the
heat. But then, just looking at Mary in that revealing
little sundress and matching jacket dispersed the chill
and made him hot all over again.

His hand deserted the steering wheel long enough to take Mary's and clamp it higher on his thigh.

She jerked her hand away.

He grabbed it back and placed the open palm nearer his knee this time.

"Hey, you two," La Jean jested, "what's with the tug of war?"

He and Mary laughed self-consciously—and then just for the pure delight of laughing, and at the prospect of the perfect evening ahead of them.

The High Lonesome was a barnlike affair twelve miles out of town, and people came from as far as a hundred miles away, which wasn't far to go, considering the scarcity of Saturday-night entertainment on the plains. A sliced-lemon moon was already balanced on the mountain peaks by the time Rafe wedged the pickup in among the welter of automobiles.

The High Lonesome was swinging. Inside the walls were studded with branding irons, saddles, barbed wire and wanted posters. The smoke-congested, music-vibrating dance hall was packed like a school bus. So, too, was the long length of a brass-railed bar that looked like something right out of a western B movie.

The country-and-western band was a good one, especially considering that it was playing at a wilderness outpost. The couples on the crowded dance floor were two-stepping their way through the sawdust to a melancholy love song that was high on the music charts.

As Rafe and Eddie searched for an empty table, friends here and there hailed the two with invitations to join them. But Rafe didn't want to share Mary with anyone. It'd be just like some drunken cowpoke who had no respect for womanhood to try to dance with her. And if anyone held her exquisite little body close, it was going to be him.

At last Eddie located a table tucked away in a dim corner. Its distance from the dance floor had let it go undetected, but at least conversation was possible that far from the band. At La Jean's pretty plea Eddie lit the small table's candle with his cigarette lighter.

A bleached-blond siren in tight denims wriggled up to take their order. As she sultrily inventoried Rafe's lean, muscular frame in the interest of future contact, her false lashes batted like fly swatters.

Idiotically, he was proud of Mary in her sizzling orange sundress. She looked so feminine, so cool in comparison, that it was all he could do to keep his hands from rollicking through that cloud of russet hair or sliding beneath that defenseless skirt. The tight V between her breasts was tantalizingly visible. So sexy, yet so untouchable. He couldn't lay one finger on her.

What he needed was a double Scotch—at once.

"Four beers," he told the siren.

While they waited for the dance floor to clear, they launched into crazy stories, jested about the dancers and their style, and drank the cold beer. Mary was enchanting. Her story about her disastrous first day as a technician when she rolled a wheelchair patient into the lavatory instead of the laboratory had them laughing hysterically.

Every time her pink tongue stole out to wipe daintily at the beer's foam on her lip, an erotic current flowed through Rafe, and he had to restrain himself from lunging forward to lap the foam off her lip for her.

After the two women excused themselves to visit the ladies' room Eddie said, "Gee, ol' friend, you got it bad."

Rafe downed his beer, a sudden morose feeling overtaking him. "Don't know what you mean."

His friend tilted his glass to his mouth, then said, "Must say, you don't seem quite the rake you were a year ago. Christina and a few others of the fair sex have been inquiring as to your whereabouts. And speaking of Christina, here she comes."

Rafe glanced up, unmoved by the sight of the beautiful woman undulating toward him. No cheap Western denims sheathed this statuesque body. Her designer jeans with a fox stitched across the back pocket attracted the glance of nearly every male she passed.

Behind her, escorting her, was Beau Brewster. "Hello, Eddie," she purred. "Rafe, darling. Imagine the two of you, bereft of dates."

"Hardly," La Jean said dryly, joining them. "The two beasties belong to us."

Christina's gaze flicked away from La Jean to slide over Mary's simple sundress with smug contempt.

Rafe looked up and caught the way Mary's eyes narrowed in instant animosity, and joy cavorted inside him at what he hoped was jealousy.

Then Beau leaned close to Mary and whispered something that made her smile.

Rafe surged out of his chair. "Let's dance," he growled, and took her by the hand, almost dragging her onto the dance floor. Let Beau and Christina console each other, he thought with annoyance.

In the strobe light Mary's eyes were very gray, and they glittered with laughter as they looked up at him. He didn't care. He noted with masculine satisfaction how when he took her in his arms everything squeezed together so perfectly—and how she was so short that he didn't have to remove his Stetson to dance with her.

As they danced his hand pressed the area below the small of her back, pushing the lower half of her torso into the hard wedge of his thigh.

"Don't do that, Rafe," she admonished.

His eyes rounded innocently. "What, honey?"

She answered by thrusting her heel punishingly into his boot, but her breasts contradicted that reply by flattening themselves against his chest. A rapturous war whoop bubbled in his throat. What a challenge. What a woman.

When they finally returned to the table after five successive dances, Eddie was nibbling La Jean's neck. Still, she was able to observe pertly, "Rafe, you look positively frazzled."

He pushed his Stetson back. "Mary's driving me crazy, La Jean."

Mary laughed with charming delight, and he hugged her tighter in the crook of his arm. He wanted to be alone with her and wished everyone would just disappear, including La Jean and Eddie, despite how much he liked them.

More stories combined with pitchers of beer were passed around the table, with acquaintances coming and going and all the males interested in meeting the soft, sexy woman with Rafe. They all wore a dazed look when Mary turned her gorgeous gray eyes on them—as if they had been slammed in the solar plexus. Her pleased amusement at their reactions only confirmed Rafe's opinion that he needed to get her away from those predatory animals and off to himself.

After what seemed forever he stowed her in the pickup—along with Eddie and La Jean. Mary's thigh nudging his was causing excruciating pleasure in his lower, combustible region. In the darkened cab his hand caressed the bare flesh of her knee just under the hem of her dress, and he heard her soft giggle, informing him that she was fully aware of his intentions. Her knees clamped shut, and his hand got no further. But at least it was there, touching the woman who was causing him such delicious torment.

Eddie and La Jean sang a riotously bawdy duet. Mary laughed at the end of each stanza, and just hearing that sweet laughter made Rafe as delirious as a lovestruck teenager on his first date.

Eddie's pickup was parked at La Jean's house, and after Rafe dropped them off, he and Mary were at last alone. Her head sought the cradle of his shoulder, and his shoulder and hand knew pure bliss for the short duration of the drive to Rancho Encantado. When he halted before her place he expected her to withdraw the delights that were temporarily his and escape into the adobe fortress. But miracles were still at work.

She offered up her sweet-scented mouth. "Rafe, kiss me good night," she murmured.

With unseemly eagerness he slid from beneath the wheel to the center of the seat. "Come here, honey," he crooned. "Let me love you."

The intense urgency curling through him would kill him in the morning, but he'd go out and buy a bottle of antacids for himself. For now . . . His mouth clamped over hers and he began kissing her. He could have been a college kid again at Harvard, parking with that special girl—whoever it was that week. But Mary had enchanted him for much longer than a week.

He liked everything about her, the way she walked, the warmth she demonstrated for other people, her love for her brother, the way she smiled, talking with her . . . damn, it was just pure pleasure holding her close, stroking the soft skin of her shoulders and arms, sucking her tongue.

He could hear his heavy breathing throbbing like a bass drum in his ears. Or was it her heavy breathing? Or both of theirs? His hand worked at the sundress's thin spaghetti straps and inched the top lower until he could cup one perfect mound. Greedily he kneaded it between his fingers, at the same time feeling his own desire rapidly rising.

His other hand began a sensuous journey up her thigh. "Don't, Rafe," she pleaded softly.

"Mary," he rasped, "you should have worked for the Spanish Inquisition. You torture so well."

His mouth absorbed her soft little mews of pleasure while his hands went wild. Her lips were hot and wet under his, and his hand continued its exploration. It was rewarded by the discovery of the satin of her panties. They pressed damply against his fingertips. Oh, heaven was near!

"Rafe . . ." She pushed against his forearm, and he could hear the panic in her voice. "I've got to go . . . you promised. Please."

Abrupt pain curdled in him. He felt like cursing, like crying. "Let's go," he managed to gasp out.

She disdained to look at him, but tugged the top of her sundress over her petulantly thrusting breasts. By the time he saw her to the door his legs were so wobbly that he didn't think he could make it back to the pickup.

Dammit, he had to be out of his mind to take this kind of treatment from her. He was out of his mind over her, period.

Mary floated into her bedroom. It had been the most marvelous evening of her life. She tossed one high-heeled sandal onto the stuffed armchair. Rafe's good friends were her friends. Another shoe fell near

the closet door. She felt expansively alive. Her panties, damp with her excitement, dropped at the foot of
the bed. He was such a gentleman. He had stopped
when she drew the line, had not tried to force his
attentions further, unlike some obnoxious dates—
who had not succeeded. Her dress slithered to the
floor. He was such a gentle man. The way he held her,
touched her. Silly, charming man, thinking he could
seduce her.

She slid beneath the sheets nude, prepared to sleep
dreamlessly.

She didn't even sleep.

She rolled from one side of the bed to the other.
She lay on her back; she rolled onto her stomach. She
kicked the rumpled linens off; she punched the pillow.
The leftover languor of the ecstatic evening was
dissipating, to be replaced by a vague sense of dissatis-
faction. An emptiness, an aching longing.

She got up and pattered to the kitchen to take two
antacids, then returned to the rumpled bed. She
muttered a curse into the flattened pillow. It was Rafe
Anaya's fault that she was in this dithered state of
mind and body—hopelessly in love with him. And she
knew that their relationship was at a stalemate. It
wouldn't go any further unless her love for Rafe was
consummated. If any man were to awaken her from
the virginal state she was suspended in, it could only
be him.

She sprang from her bed. Now that her mind was
made up, she couldn't do it quickly enough. As she
finished dressing her hands fumbled nervously with

the sundress's zipper. Outside the stars were bright and hot and lit the way for the Mustang.

Only when she reached Rafe's front door did she realize what a silly thing she was doing. Worse, she was compromising herself. She firmly believed in a commitment between one man and one woman. And Rafe believed in the old notches-on-the-gun-handle system.

She retreated a step in preparation for flight, but by then it was too late. Rafe opened the door and flipped on the porch light. His hair was disheveled, and he, too, was in his bare feet. He was shirtless, and his jeans were unsnapped. "Mary," he said dumbly.

She gathered her courage and said, "Rafe, I love you . . . and . . . and I want you to show me the love you promised could be so beautiful."

Bemused, he could only stare at her—until she reached out with one hand to touch his bare chest. "I'm nervous, Rafe," she whispered. "Please say something."

"Mary, this is a damned poor joke at this time of night."

She caught his hand, afraid he would resist now that she had finally gathered her courage, and pulled him along the hallway. A maze of expensively appointed rooms slid by her peripheral vision as she made the long journey toward his bedroom.

He stopped her at the bedroom's doorway. "Mary, what do you think you're doing? You'll only be sorry later."

The heat of his hand was on her arm, and she

whirled to face him. "All this time you wanted to make love to me, Rafe. You aren't changing your mind now that I want you to, are you?"

He blinked, then stalked past her into his bedroom, snapping his jeans as he went. As if forgetting her presence, he prowled the large room. At last, jamming his hands into his jeans' back pockets, he confronted her. "You can't just demand that a man perform at the snap of your fingers. Good Lord, Mary, what's gotten into that lovely, zany mind of yours?"

Before his fierce expression—the brown eyes dark with both agitation and confusion, the mouth hard and unrelenting—her grand scheme began to crumble. The mugs of beer must have addled her head. Shame crawled over her, leaving its blushing red track.

She whirled from him and buried her face in the palms of her hands. "Oh, Rafe," she groaned, "it's all your fault. I never was like this before you intruded into my life. I wasn't featherbrained. I was practical and logical, with a serious—"

His kiss, hot and sweet, on her nape silenced her. He turned her to face him, holding her tightly, pressing her head against his chest. She felt him shudder beneath her cheek. "Oh, honey, honey, you feel so good." The spaces where their two bodies didn't touch radiated with the heat arcing between them. "Mary, I've waited so long for you that I'm just as nervous as you are."

"I know, I know." She was in a desperate rush to get it over with.

But he wasn't. He wanted to go slow, to make it good for her. "There's no hurry, Mary."

She smiled, but he could sense the strain behind her smile. "All right, how slow do we go?"

"This slow." He tipped her chin up so that his mouth could claim hers in a kiss that was surprisingly tender. He made no effort to invade her mouth, yet his sweet kiss stirred in her a response that left her wanting more. And she made no objection when he inched her body away from his and slipped the sundress's thin straps over her bare shoulders and tugged the bodice down.

"Yes . . . yes," she murmured when his hands gently, almost reverently lifted her breasts.

"Mary, sweet, you're so lovely," he choked out thickly.

His fingers traced each dusky areola before his head dipped and his mouth, warm and wet, encircled a nipple that was wrinkled with excitement. The current of sudden wanting waved through her, leaving her weak, so that she had to clutch at his hips to keep from sagging.

"Please, Rafe," she begged.

"I can't wait any longer either, love." He was unzipping her dress in a frenzied haste. The dress floated to her feet. When his arms slid around her shoulders and under the back of her legs to lift her high against him, she thought: At last! Carrying her to his bed, he kissed her with a savage hunger that thrilled her, before he discarded his jeans.

She was intensely aware of his nakedness, feverish against her own blazing skin. Beneath her hands she could feel the flex of the smooth muscles in his back. He was a powerful—and heavy—man. And his pent-up impatience excited her. Until he slid up over her. Then a chill of detachment settled over her. Her limbs refused to operate.

His hands slid beneath her to grip the rounded mounds of her rear, anchoring her to him. His mouth claimed hers, and he breathed against her lips, "I've waited so long for you, Mary!" Then, almost as if he were cursing himself, "God help me, I can't wait any longer. I can't help myself."

The preliminaries of his lovemaking lost their erotically exciting effect on her when he took her with the hot impatience of pure lust. His knee jammed between her thighs, and he slid into her, halted at the barrier, then plunged deeply.

Unfortunately, her mind *was* functioning. Analytically she experienced the loss of her virginity—that first stab of pain that subsided somewhat with the acceleration of the act. Now she could identify with that vulnerability that only a woman could know. She stifled her initial whimper at the back of her throat.

From what seemed like a great distance she could hear Rafe's heavy breathing, whispering his need of her and other passionate words that a man whispers to a woman, words that she had never heard.

She forced her hands to unclench and hold his back.

Soon it would be over, she told herself, her disappointment thudding in tempo with the deep hammering within her. Then she could go home. If only he'd get it over with. He did, the rhythm of his movements accelerating quickly before he shuddered to a stop.

He lay there, still buried inside her, his hunger only incompletely satisfied. He felt her impatient wiggle beneath him. "Mary, honey," he whispered huskily, "I'm sorry." He rolled from her and began to stroke her cold face with grave concern. "I didn't even last long enough to take care of you."

She sat up, mechanically tucking in the hair that had torn loose from its knot. Dazed with wrenching disappointment, she slipped from the tangle of sheets and reached for her dress. "It's all right, Rafe."

He uncoiled from the bed with a swiftness that startled her. "It's not all right, dammit!" His hands caught her shoulders and jerked her around to face him. "It's supposed to be an exciting experience! I botched it, Mary. I couldn't stop."

She shrugged her shoulders. "I'm going now."

"No, Mary." His face was impassioned, anguished. "Don't. Stay. Let me show you that it can be beautiful. I was in too much of a hurry. Please, Mary, this isn't the way it's supposed to be."

She pulled away. "I smell of your lovemaking, Rafe. How many other women have you imbued with that secret odor?"

She saw that her words were like a slap in the face. "Many," he acknowledged baldly. "You're the first woman I wanted so badly to enjoy it with me."

She didn't bother to zip her dress, just started listlessly down the long hallway. Her limbs seemed so heavy. Rafe caught up with her. "Mary, I'm not into scoring on virgins. What I wanted to happen between us was more than just sex. I wanted us to make love."

She wrenched away.

"At least let me drive you home."

She shook her head. "No, I'll be all right."

And she was, she thought as she wheeled the Mustang through the moonlit night. She knew now what copulation was. And she knew now that she was over her sensual, erotic infatuation with Rafe.

Yet his smell—the sweet, musky scent—bathed her thighs and pervaded the car. She was one of his many women, and she knew, try as she might, that she would not forget that smell. For the rest of her life it would tantalize her.

Rafe swore with feeling and eloquence. He paced the patio, his nude body glistening with the aftersweat of lovemaking. He yanked the cigarette from his mouth and tossed it out into the night. Its red glow made an arc and then disappeared. The outburst of profanity had made him feel a little bit better.

He had possessed Mary, and now this wanting of her would be finished. He felt a curious relief. He thought about Christina. She had been a willing bed partner who moaned orgiastically. Or Lisa in El Paso. The divorcée had been more acrobatic in bed than the Olympic tumbling team.

Hell! He reached for another cigarette from the

package on the patio table. With the second cigarette, inhaling deeply, a semblance of ordered thought infused his mind.

He was genuinely amazed by his intense reaction to Mary. And with the lucidity that often follows exhilaration he was forced to face the depressingly unpleasant fact that, with the possession of her, his interest in her had not waned.

He loved her more than ever.

Chapter 11

HERMALINDA LIFTED HER HEAD FROM THE TABLE WHERE she was lying and grinned. *"Hola, soltera."*

Mary shut the examination room's door behind her. "Hello, Hermalinda," she said in a carefully schooled professional voice.

She didn't want the young woman to know that she had been worried about her two-month lapse in visiting the clinic. The cagey Hermalinda would know how to use her concern, how to slyly turn it into a weakness that would benefit herself, come time for the baby's delivery.

Mary picked up the chart on the counter, glancing through the brief history. "So, how do you feel, Hermalinda?"

The Indian woman giggled, and her red, roughened hand patted the stomach that resembled a miniature

domed stadium. "I feel stuffed like a *piñata, soltera*—
and ready to break open, just so."

Mary contained the smile that threatened to erupt
at the woman's freshness. The pregnant women of
Washington's *haut monde* who patronized the Scott-
Waggoner Medical Complex would have complained
of myriad ills and failed to see the humor in this
temporary state of the body.

She took Hermalinda's blood pressure, noting its
slight increase. Next she performed the pelvic examination. The uterus was large and distended even for
the last trimester. "I hope it's a *piñata* and not
yourself you've been stuffing, Hermalinda."

"Well, maybe a little I eat."

The swollen fingers and ankles suggested fluid
retention. Not a good sign. "Let's see just how little.
Step on the scales."

With the disposable gown held in place over her
bulging abdomen, the woman waddled over to the
scales. Mary shifted the weights. An eleven-pound
gain. The gain, added to the distended pelvis,
strengthened her opinion that Hermalinda could possibly be carrying twins. That was dangerous in a
woman with such a narrow pelvis.

"Hermalinda," she lectured sternly, "you must
watch your weight. You could get *eclampsia*—toxic
poisoning."

The woman's square face furrowed. "Poisoning?"

"Too much protein in the urine. I'm going to give
you some medicine to take. A diuretic to control the
swelling. Also, you are not to use salt on your food."

"*¡Ejoli!*" The woman stepped off the scales hastily. "No salt?"

"No salt. And one more thing. Is there a history . . . does anyone in your family have twins?"

"Twins?" Hermalinda searched in her memory; then her face lightened. "Ahhh, *sí, mi tía*—my mother's sister, Dolores."

"I think your joke about carrying twins may have been accurate. Everything indicates the possibility of more than one child."

"*¡Ay de mí!*" She genuflected quickly. "I am truly blessed."

All things considered, Mary would have questioned that blessing—especially when, an hour later, Hanson's uniformed bulk filled her office doorway.

"Yes?" she asked coolly.

The Border Patrol agent lumbered over to her desk and settled his massive thigh on the corner of the desktop. Behind him La Jean signaled her impotence in blocking the man's entrance with a helpless shrug of her shoulders and rolled her eyes ceilingward.

Hanson tipped his hat. It was a mockery of chivalry. His kind had no respect for womanhood—or anything but the power of brute strength. Her image in his silvered sunglasses reflected her contemptuous expression.

"Here on duty, Doc. Just picked up the pregnant Mex for the second time. Next arrest, it'll be her third strike. I'll make sure the Immigration Department buries her for a long time in La Tuna."

La Tuna was the federal prison near El Paso, and Mary knew Hanson would make good on his word of incarcerating Hermalinda. She shivered but asked evenly, "What do you want with me?"

"You're making it damned hard for me to do my job, Doc." He fingered the folder still on her desk—bearing Hermalinda's name. "To my way of thinking, the NHSC wouldn't like to find out their employee was treating illegal aliens."

She eyed him coldly. "Merely observing—not treating, Hanson."

"Merely warning," he parodied with a mean smile. "Not arresting."

She rose in a gesture of dismissal. "You've done your duty, then."

He took the hint and rose also. "If I catch you in the act, Doc, I'll see to it that you never lift a scalpel, much less hang out your shingle to practice, again. Do you understand me?"

"My clinic has been sterilized against vermin, so please leave."

He tipped his hat again. "Sorry you have to take offense, Doc." His eyes said otherwise, that he took pleasure in her discomfort.

After he left she slumped back down in her chair. Did anything ever go right? She closed her eyes in weary astonishment at this latest turn of events.

La Jean came into the office, spraying the room with a can of disinfectant. "For the vermin!" She laughed.

Mary groaned and rubbed her temples, wishing she could rub away the last visitor. "The vermin's merely a new low in an already hellish week."

"The river of love not flowing smoothly?" La Jean asked solicitously.

Mary's head snapped up, and her insides winced at the memory of the pain she had known when she had thought to feel joy. "Has Eddie said anything—about Rafe?"

La Jean chewed thoughtfully on her gum. "Only that Rafe was as bristly as a porcupine when he mentioned double-dating again this weekend."

As she had waited for that answer, Mary had felt like she was looking down the barrel of a rifle. What if Rafe had been the kind to spread the word of his latest coup—making it with a virgin, with "the spinster"? It would have hurt her more than the fact that he hadn't bothered to call her or try to see her since that night. Maybe the disastrous affair had been all her fault. Maybe she was just a cold, uptight spinster after all. Maybe she just didn't have what it took to satisfy a man.

La Jean touched her shoulder. "Mary, be patient with Rafe. He's got to get used to the idea of love."

"Who said anything about love?"

"I may not be a doctor, Mary, but I can sure diagnose a case of lovesickness."

"A case of lovesickness is something I don't have time for," Mary said with a finality that discouraged further word on the subject.

And yet she was imbecilic enough to love Rafe

wildly, almost beyond herself. She loved everything about him, his strengths—which included his deep concern for other people—and his weaknesses, which were his male pride and fear of permanency. But she would not make the mistake of going to him again. She had failed to provide stimulating lovemaking for Kingdom Come's stud, and he was no doubt partaking of womanly favors elsewhere.

She buried her lacerated feelings in her work, not even taking time for lunch, for the clinic's waiting room these last few weeks was seating a growing number of patients. True, it wasn't so packed that the patients were forced to stand, but the trickle had become a steady stream—mostly those from Kingdom Come's small middle-class community, including those people she had met through Rafe: W. H. Delbert, the lawyer, Barbara, the barber, and the others.

When she had seen the three remaining appointments for the day, she made up her mind that she wasn't going to sit around the adobe and mope for the rest of her term in Kingdom Come. Instead, she went shopping at the small dress shop on Kingdom Come's main street and found just what she needed to perk her up. She drove home, bathed and changed into the ice-green crepe-and-lace dress that floated about her legs.

Since she had missed lunch she would take herself out to the Oasis for dinner, and she would have a good time! The Oasis was crowded by the time she got there—or rather its bar was, mostly with men in boots and jeans, with cans of beer in their hands. A few women, the usual sultry barflies, studded the stools.

She sashayed past the bar's entrance, her little chin tucked in the air with supreme confidence she did not feel, and found a booth to herself in the restaurant portion. A scattering of couples and two or three families occupied several booths and tables. Desultorily she looked over the menu and settled on chicken-fried steak just about the time Beau Brewster slid into the seat opposite her. He was dressed like a typical urban cowboy, right down to the pearl snaps on his Western shirt.

"'Evening, Mary. You dining alone?"

She didn't feel particularly hospitable, but when Rafe and Eddie, out of uniform, walked in at that moment, the corners of her lips curled in an inviting smile directed at Beau. "It would appear that way."

From the corner of her eye she saw Rafe scowl, and ignored him. He stalked on into the bar, and she forced herself to pay attention to Beau's flirtatious banter during the meal. But it was difficult when she heard tinkling feminine laughter from the bar. The Don Juan louse. She fished in her purse for an antacid and concentrated even harder on the discussion at hand—something about a citywide cleanup campaign that Beau said the bank was mounting.

As he talked Beau found it difficult to take his eyes off that fascinating little face. His gaze fastened on her curving mouth, and he could feel a shudder of desire ripple through him.

Mary sat almost unaware of him. Every so often

she caught the edges of Rafe's low laughter. She eyed the dim bar section sourly.

Beau intercepted the look. "You want an after-dinner drink, Mary?" She was intoxicating enough that he was already drunk just watching her.

"Yes!" she answered with alacrity.

The bar was dim. Two stools were vacant along the U-shaped bar—across from Eddie and Rafe. A saucy little brunette with a bust that was anything but little sat by Rafe's side. She had apparently been unsuccessful in her seductive bid for his attention if the sullen pout on her overripe lips was any indication.

Rafe looked up from the can of beer he seemed to be intently investigating. "Well, hel-lo, Mary," he said in an innocent tone of surprise.

Her fingers curled in an itchy desire to leave their imprint on the other woman's cheek as she toyed with Rafe's rolled-up sleeve. Mary smiled sweetly. "Well, hel-lo, Rafe."

Eddie looked from his friend to Mary and back to his friend, then resumed nursing his private thoughts in the privacy of his beer. The fireworks were coming.

"What are you doing here?" Rafe asked.

"What are *you* doing here?" she returned.

"Drinking the Oasis dry."

"What happened to your green tea?" she purred, her eyes wide.

"Started tasting like coyote pellets," he muttered, and took another swig of beer.

Beau ordered two beers, sensing that once more Mary was completely oblivious of his presence. On

one hand his masculinity was affronted. On the other
—it simply didn't matter. He was sitting next to this
tantalizing little ice maiden, wasn't he? With patience,
who knew what might happen? One by one he
cracked his knuckles.

When Mary tipped her beer to her mouth and
licked the foam off one corner of her lips in that
characteristic but unintentionally provocative gesture,
Beau laughed delightedly and brushed away the foam
glistening at her lips' other corner with his forefinger.

Rafe lunged off the stool. "Come on, Mary, you're
going home."

Beau came to his feet. "Just a minute, Rafe. I
didn't hear Mary say anything about wanting to
leave."

She jumped when Rafe's fingers manacled her wrist
in a possessive grip. In the bar's dimness his eyes
glittered like gold in the palm of a greedy man's hand.
His glare would have killed quicker than a first frost
killed flies. "Sorry, ol' friend," he said in a dangerously quiet voice that had lost its slur, "but this one
belongs to me."

The conversation along the length of the U-shaped
bar stopped in the suddenly cold atmosphere. Mary
stood between the two men, who sized each other up.
Rafe was the taller and brawnier, but Beau looked
solid enough to hold his own. The animosity that
crackled in the air was exciting, but she was too
worried to enjoy the moment of two knights vying for
her hand.

"Rafe," Eddie intervened, "your beer's going flat."

"Maybe you want your friend's help," Beau taunted, losing the patience he had carefully cultivated as part of his banker's image.

Rafe's eyes narrowed like those of a flagged bull. "I'm going to kill you, you son of a—"

"Rafe!" Mary warned. "I'm quite capable of taking care of myself. I came in my own car, and I'll leave in my own car, thank you."

With all the dignity of royalty she sailed majestically out of the barroom, leaving the two stupefied opponents to watch her depart.

She swore all the way home.

The next day, Saturday, she launched frenetically into a whirlwind of housework, beginning with flushing Rafe's green tea and her own antacids down the toilet. She didn't plan to let him invade her life and upset her existence again.

When she drove into town to restock her kitchen shelves, Vicente greeted her heartily. "Hey, *soltera,* you come for green tea, no?"

"No!" She grabbed a shopping cart that was ready for the recycling plant. It rattled over the uneven concrete floor. "I have come for sensible foods, Vicente. Milk. Eggs. Cheese. Bread."

The fat little man scratched his balding head, puzzled by *la soltera's* abrupt reply.

She wheeled the cart into the dairy aisle, where she bumped into Carmelita, who was filling a rounded wire basket with eggs. At the young woman's side was her son, who clung pathetically to her gaily colored calico skirt.

Irritation at the young woman washed over Mary. Irritation, rather, at her backwardness that permitted a child's crossed eyes to go untreated. And there was not a little envy mixed in, Mary thought honestly, however reluctantly. Envy for the beautiful young woman whom Rafe treated with such gentleness.

She ruffled the boy's curly brown hair. "Hello, Lucero. Carmelita."

The boy kept his gaze trained on the cracked concrete floor. Carmelita nodded shyly and slipped past, tugging Lucero after her. Mary watched them hurry away. Her shoulders slumped with the impotence she felt. What was she doing there in Kingdom Come, trying to convince people who wanted no part of her that she could help them?

It was as if her blood had suddenly been depleted of its energy. She returned home to mope about the adobe with an inertia that was uncharacteristic of her. Then her gaze fell on the monthly medical journal that had finally caught up with her change-of-address that afternoon. The cover featured Albert Schweitzer, who had combated ignorance, prejudice and primitive conditions to serve the African people for over forty years.

Could she do less in a mere six months of hardship? Especially when Schweitzer's first clinic had been a chicken coop, no less?

Chickens were what she encountered when, on Monday afternoon, she made a third visit to Josefita's house. The *curandera* was in the yard, and chickens poked at the sun-baked earth while she fed them grain that she toted in her bunched apron.

Mary got out of the Mustang and crossed the dirt yard. "Can I talk with you for a minute, Josefita?"

The old woman eyed her from beneath her fierce brows. "What can you say? All has been said."

"No. Not all." From her purse she produced a pamphlet on ocular muscle imbalance. "Josefita, if your grandson is not treated early enough for his crossed eyes, he could lose his sight. Look here, at the diagram. With glasses—or by covering the good eye—and ocular muscle exercises, with a little luck we can correct the problem without surgery. After six years of age, though, surgery is almost always required."

Josefita studied the drawings for a moment, then turned indifferently back to her chickens. "I will use my own *remedios*."

Mary lost her cool. "And what happens when your *remedios* fail to cure your grandson's eyes?"

The old woman paused to look at Mary. The rheumy eyes never blinked. "Then we pray."

"Pray? Hell, no! Then we perform surgery."

"You will be driven from town first," Josefita said flatly, firmly.

Mary sat beneath a golden cottonwood for she didn't know how long. She watched the slow, timeless drift of the Rio Grande. Every so often the evening breeze rustled the tree limbs and a few leaves fluttered onto the sloping bank, reminders that it was late autumn. High above, a jet banked, arcing toward El Paso, and the dying sunlight winked off its wings.

Twilight was shadowing the view of the river, and with a sigh she rose, making her way back to the parked Mustang. The time she had spent on the riverbank in reflection had defused her agitation over the confrontation with Josefita.

When she walked into her living room it was dark. Immediately she halted just inside the door. A sixth sense, woman's intuition perhaps, told her that she was not alone in the room. The fine hairs on her nape prickled. After a fleeting but agonizing moment while she recalled the vandalized clinic, Hanson's threat, Josefita's calm anger, she asked cautiously, "Who's there?"

The lamp's light flooded the room. Rafe sat in the overstuffed chair, hunched forward, his hands interlocked between his knees. She didn't know which appeared more rumpled—his Western shirt or his thick hair. His expression looked wretched.

"How did you get in?" she breathed.

"I'm your landlord, remember?"

"I've never forgotten," she said dryly, bitterly.

"Come here, Mary."

She tensed. "What do you want?"

"You—unfortunately." He came to his feet, and she saw all the strength of his people embodied in him. "Mary, I've made such a mess of everything. I want to try again."

"You aren't here just because your male ego is smarting over your last performance?" she snapped.

He raked his fingers through his hair. "I've gone out several times since the night you came to my house. Once I picked up a woman, and I—"

She swept past him, saying, "And you made love to her."

His hand grabbed her elbow, halting her. She looked up into his anguished face and tried to harden herself against him.

"That's just it, Mary. I couldn't." His mouth curled in a self-deprecating smile. "I tried, but there was nothing there. I simply didn't want to make love to her. That's what I want to do to you. With you. Desperately. Desperately enough to let you call all the shots."

She couldn't meet the intensity of those deep-set eyes. He would surely see the wanting in her own. She looked past him into the darkened hallway. "Rafe, what happens between us—no good can come of it. I'm not good at your sort of game, at indiscriminate sex."

His hands cupped her shoulders as if he never wanted to let her go again. "I don't want indiscriminate sex, Mary. I want you. Only you."

It sounded dangerously close to a marriage proposal. And it frightened her, because she knew Rafe would never leave Kingdom Come. And she would never stay.

He relieved her anxiety, saying, "Will you give us a chance to make your remaining months in Kingdom Come good for each other? I want a commitment between us, Mary. I don't want to have to worry

about killing every man who puts his arms about you
while you're here."

"What about Christina?"

"Mary, sweet, I haven't been to bed with her since
you hit Kingdom Come and disrupted its placid
existence."

"And the lovemaking between us?"

His fingers tightened on her flesh, and beneath the
handlebar mustache his smile was wry. "If you demand that I behave like a Trappist monk, I'll do it.
Yet I'm so delirious just to see you, to touch you—
hell, even just kiss you. But, oh, Mary, I want so
damn much more!"

She did. And she didn't. She wanted him to hold
her again, his hands cruising over her body, weighing
her uptilted breasts, investigating her secret places.
But she was reluctant to think beyond that point.

She turned her lips to meet his hungry kiss. His
hands were greedily fondling her breasts, and when he
drew back she did not stay the fingers that fumbled
feverishly at her blouse's buttons and the bra's snap.
Then her breasts were freed, naked to his touch.

"Lovely . . . lovely," he groaned, his fingers trem-
ulously pulling at the dusky nipples, coaxing. His head
dipped to gently bite one, and her hands stiffened
against his shoulders in apprehension.

"It's all right, honey. I'll go slow, let you set the
pace." Gently he kissed first one nipple and then the
other and tucked her breasts back into the bra's lacy
cups.

Watching him, she thought she'd melt. She didn't

want him to stop, to leave her aching for more like this. But what if it was the same painful, sticky, sweaty act as before? Instinctively she knew that if it happened again, she couldn't fool him. He was too experienced to know a feigned reaction.

Worse, if their lovemaking were the incredible beauty that songs and poems promised, it would be that much more difficult for her when the time came for her to leave.

Chapter 12

RAFE'S EXCITING TOUCH NEVER CEASED TO BE A WONDER to Mary's starved body. As the days of November drifted by and Rafe slowly seduced her with his hotly passionate kisses and his almost savagely hungry hands, she knew a kind of frustration she had never experienced before.

Her stomach protested constantly, seeming to feed on itself. And while Rafe was the essence of a gentleman, she sometimes caught the testiness in his voice. She sensed that his restraint was wearing thin. Seeing each other as often as they did, all hours of the day and night, they both ended up with too little sleep and too much work—and nerves that were stretched far too taut.

Eddie and Le Jean's courtship didn't seem plagued by those inner tensions and nagging subconscious questions that seeped into Rafe and Mary's relationship. When La Jean announced that Eddie had asked her to marry him, Mary was thrilled for her. "You told me your children were wild about Eddie. They must be happy about a Christmas wedding."

With a hearty chuckle La Jean plopped her lanky frame in the swivel chair. "Delirious. We all are." She leaned her elbows on her desk and propped her chin in her hands. "You know, Mary, you and Rafe ought to give the institution a chance."

The word "institution" reminded Mary of the Lea County Institution for Indigents, where she had spent many a night as a child. "I don't think so, La Jean. Kingdom Come's star bachelor has his own feelings about marriage, which I doubt coincide with most people's."

Irritably she wondered how she could possibly be entertaining the idea of marriage. What was she thinking? Even if Rafe were willing to shackle himself in the bonds of marriage, she couldn't see herself marooned in an abandoned community like Kingdom Come for the rest of her life, unable to practice the profession she had trained for, yearned for, for so many years. She was meant to be a doctor. She was a good doctor. But she'd never get the chance to prove it in Kingdom Come.

Decisively she put Rafe and the future from her mind and went back to work. Later that day she examined Al, a railroad man. He had degenerative arthritis affecting the knee area, and as she walked him to the outer office she prescribed remedial treatment. "Weight reduction will help, Al. Also local heat and massage. But it'd be wise to avoid stair climbing and—"

She broke off as Rafe closed the clinic door none too gently behind him. Startled, La Jean looked up from the receipt she was making out, and the railroad man's knees almost buckled with surprise at the door's slam. "Rafe," Mary said, "what is—?"

"Pack your overnight bag, Mary. We're spending Thanksgiving Day in El Paso. At my grandmother's."

"Thanksgiving?" she repeated stupidly. Since Billy had written that he would be deer hunting near Cloudcroft over the holidays, and Amy had mentioned she would be having Thanksgiving dinner with her roommate's family, Mary had forgotten about the holiday.

"Take her away, Rafe," La Jean cheered. "I'll close up the office."

He drove her to the adobe and paced like a caged bobcat while she reluctantly packed a suitcase. She didn't want to meet his grandmother; she didn't want to learn any more about Rafe; she didn't want to do anything that might bind her to him more tightly than she already was.

"My plants," she hedged at the door. "Who'll water my plants?"

The ends of his mustache jutted downward. "Mary, we're only going to be gone for a day and a night."

"Does your grandmother know you're bringing me?"

He groaned. "Yes, Mary."

"What about emergencies at the clinic?"

Patience gone, he grabbed the suitcase from her hand and took her arm in a firm grasp. "Shall I put it in the Kingdom Come newspaper: 'Rafe Anaya has temporarily abducted Dr. Mary Margulies for the purpose of seduction. She will be back to work Friday at regular business hours'?"

A couple of seconds were all she could manage before she broke into laughter. Once the MG was on the road she turned to him and asked, "Are you really abducting me for that purpose—seduction?"

He took his eyes off the highway long enough for his heated gaze to touch her lips, her breasts and her thighs, shielded by her smart khaki trousers. "I don't know, Mary," he bit out. "You've got me so damned confused, I'm behaving like a Keystone Kop."

She grinned, and he said, "Ahh, Mary, can I help it if I want to make love to you so badly?"

"At your grandmother's house?" she teased, slightly shocked by the idea.

"Anywhere I can, honey." His free hand played with the willful tendrils at her neck. Then, as if it couldn't control itself, it slid along her shoulder to seek the bare skin of her arm. "Mary, sweet, you've got the softest skin. I'd love to explore—"

"Your parents," she intervened. "Where are they?"

He groaned again at her obvious ploy, but answered, "In Spain. Dad's a diplomatic attaché at the embassy in Madrid. I guess the family has been posted at almost every embassy on the European continent at one time or another, including Lichtenstein."

"So you've traveled all over the world?"

"Not always. Sometimes my father was posted in small countries like Dubai that didn't have boarding schools above the elementary level. Then I was sent to live with my grandmother. Mostly I lived at Rancho Encantado and went to school in Kingdom Come, but after I reached high school Grandmother moved permanently to her home in El Paso. She wanted to be nearer all the functions and organizations with which she's been involved forever."

There was still so much about Rafe that she didn't know! And shouldn't know. Knowing would only make leaving Kingdom Come that much more difficult.

His hand deserted her shoulder to stroke her thigh. "You'd best keep both hands on the wheel, Rafe Anaya," she teased.

He didn't. And she thought that if he continued with his sensual ministrations she'd be begging him to make love to her before they could reach El Paso. Fortunately, after three abortive attempts he left his hand where she put it—on the steering wheel.

El Paso del Norte was a four-hundred-year-old city steeped in history and surrounded by the Rocky Mountains. The Pass of the North had always been a meeting place for conquistadors and colonists, wild Indians and devoted friars, trappers, traders and forty-niners. A crossroads for gunmen and gamblers, cavalrymen and fancy women.

And something told her that beautiful autumn day that she was at her own crossroads.

Driving through the Indian/Hispanic outskirts of Ysleta and Socorro and Tigua, she sensed some of what made up Rafe Anaya. His fierce pride, his strongly masculine nature, his gentleness and gaiety.

When they ate a late lunch at an outdoor café in Juárez she could see those same characteristics in the Mexican woman who sold tamales before Juárez's ancient Guadalupe Cathedral; in the haughty face of the old Spanish *hidalgo* who strolled with his ivory-knobbed cane in the plaza; in the faces of the olive-skinned children with dark, laughing eyes.

And in that old-world face of Rafe's grandmother, Ysabel Anaya. From her Rafe must have gotten his Hispanic's thin-bladed nose and gold-flecked eyes, though in Ysabel Anaya age had dimmed their intense hue. Her soft silver-white hair tempered the power of the spirit evident in her square chin and shrewd gaze.

She greeted them warmly at the Moorish entrance of her two-story stucco home in El Paso's old, aristocratic section, Sunset Heights. Here homes fit for Spanish grandees roled over estates instead of mere grassy yards. Mary tried not to show her nervousness before this majestic woman. She had intentionally chosen to wear a simple beige blouse and pleated khaki trousers. Somehow it seemed important to her not to put too much emphasis on this meeting.

Ysabel clasped Mary's two hands in a strong grip between her age-spotted ones. The two women were of the same height. "My child, I am so pleased that Rafe has brought you for the holiday. I'm afraid I get so testy hobnobbing only with old biddies."

"Thank you for allowing us to share Thanksgiving with you," Mary replied politely.

Ysabel flicked an eagle's piercing eye at her grandson. "He's been very remiss in keeping me abreast of his extracurricular activities."

With a teasing gleam in his eyes, Rafe bent from his great height to kiss her powdered cheek. "Now, Grandmother, I doubt whether you would have approved of some of the *gringas* I could have brought home. They didn't have your and Mary's old-world charm."

The statement surprised Mary. She thought of herself as thoroughly modern, a progressive, liberated woman with a doctor's degree. Or had she assimilated some of her mother's European culture without being aware of it?

Rafe led her up a white marble staircase to the bedroom that would be hers, a beautiful room done in blue and white, with white wicker furniture to offset the heavy wooden ceiling beams and massive door frames.

"It's lovely, Rafe."

He sat her suitcase down and took her by the shoulders, turning her to face him. "You're lovely. And I wish I could keep my hands off you."

His lips were nibbling little urgent kisses along her

neck while his hands sought to explore the curvature of her hips. "Rafe! Your grandmother might—"

"I've already told her I brought you here to make love to you," he whispered against her lips, and then began his seduction of her mouth with hot, wet little kisses that were driving her mad.

At last he set her from him, and she wondered if her knees could support her. "Want to hear the fat lady sing?" he teased.

She wanted him to continue kissing her. "Now what are you talking about?"

"Grandmother has prime seats for the El Paso Symphony Orchestra tonight. Come to think of it, the fat lady doesn't sing, but if I remember correctly the orchestra has some big bassoon players. Put on something slinky for Mozart—and me."

Mary showered quickly, only to discover that her bath connected her bedroom with Rafe's when she opened the shower door and found him leaning against the counter, arms crossed, and a sly smile on his face. He was quite naked.

Quickly she shut the glass door. "Go away!"

"I can't, honey. I've got to shower too."

Before she could frame a reply he had the door open and had stepped inside with her, backing her against the wet tile wall. His body blotted out all else. All she could say was, "Oh, Rafe!"

He took out the pins in her hair, dropping them carelessly on the shower floor. "Mary, if you don't let me make love to you soon, it's going to kill me." His hands tunneled through the heavy curtain of untamable curls, spreading them down over her wet shoulders, while his hands continued their downward journey along her rib cage, around her waist to curve around the luscious mounds of her hips. "And if I do make love to you, I'm afraid I'll never want to stop—and that will kill me."

He was kissing her, and she could feel his excitement against her soft belly. He was her bronze conquistador, come to conquer her.

When his fingers touched the delicate crevice between her legs she tensed with the spasms of something primitive. "Rafe," she murmured, "I don't think I can be any good for us."

"Oh, Mary, you excite me so." He raised his head and looked deep into her eyes. "But I won't hurt you again, love. I only want to caress you—everywhere, every lovable inch of you."

Taking the bar of soap, he pressed her against the slippery tile wall and began to tenderly lave the soft, flat stretch of her belly and beyond.

"I've already bathed," she said, her hand clutching at the one that insinuated itself between her thighs.

"I'm only leaving you something to remember me by," he whispered against her throat while the work-callused fingers of one hand lathered the soap in her downy curls. "Kiss me, Mary. You know how."

Her hands cupped his jaws, and her mouth played over his as lightly as a morning mist. She was half-afraid of what she was doing, knowing that there could be no halting at this point. She should not have feared, for Rafe would not let her excite him beyond control. She was forced to surrender, her head thrown back against the wet tile, her eyes closed, when his hand brought her to a shuddering climax.

After a long moment, when their labored breathing was the only sound to be heard, she opened her eyes, just barely, and looked at him through the sweep of her lashes. She was embarrassed. She was inexperienced and new at this, and he was so practiced.

Yet he had refrained from gratifying himself. He was still allowing her the prerogative of making the choice—but trying like mad to influence her over to his side. "Mary?"

She understood the question deep in the eyes that were shadowed by water-spiked lashes. "Thank you, Rafe," she whispered. Would her heart ever stop this stampeding gallop?

He looked terribly pleased. Water glistened in his mustache, and his teeth gleamed in an affectionate smile. A loving smile? "At this rate, we'll never get ready. I'll let you escape this time."

"I have the distinct feeling that I don't think I did," she said weakly.

Driving his grandmother's hearselike black Lincoln, Rafe took them to dinner at the plush International Club atop the State National Bank Tower. To Mary's awe, a private room had been reserved for the Anaya family. The colorful dining room's gorgeous panoramic view was this side of paradise, revealing the glittering diamonds that were El Paso and Juárez at night.

During dinner Ysabel Anaya told amusing and affectionate stories of her grandson's wicked ways as a child, to Mary's laughing appreciation.

"He hasn't changed, Mrs. Anaya," she said. Over the rim of her wineglass her eyes teased Rafe. "I'm afraid your grandson's still just as wicked."

"And I thought after he came back from Vietnam he had reformed," his grandmother sighed.

"Between the two of you," Rafe laughed, "I feel like I'm in Nam and under attack all over again."

The El Paso Symphony Orchestra performed at the modernistic Civic Center, and their delivery of Mozart held Mary spellbound—or perhaps it was the way Rafe casually stroked her palm in delicious concentric circles. On his other side his grandmother nodded in delight to the music—and in delight at Rafe and Mary. The sixteen-year-old girl's twinkle in the grandmother's seventy-year-old eyes reminded Mary of Father John.

Most of the symphony patrons looked dressed for a night in the Monte Carlo gambling casinos, with the women wearing long, elegant gowns and white gloves and the men dressed like Rafe—in black tuxedos and white formal jackets that made them look like ads for expensive Scotch or bourbon. Yet Mary's one classy outfit, the black crepe cocktail dress with the white ruffles down the plunging V neck, certainly held its own—or at least held Rafe's lusty gaze.

By midnight they returned to Sunset Heights in time for Ysabel to drink her hot milk and retire to her bedroom just beyond the old-fashioned kitchen that was replete with a beehive oven tucked in one corner.

"What?" Mary asked Rafe when he switched off the kitchen light. "No hot green tea?"

The light filtering in from the stairway glinted on his bandit's face, reckless with his wanting. "I'm already hot, honey. The whites of my eyes are turning yellow with the strain of abstinence."

"Unusual for a man of your active prowess, I would imagine."

"I'm thinking of donating that part of my atrophied body to medical science," he sighed, but a warm, teasing sparkle glinted in his eyes.

His large hand cupped one shoulder and propelled her up the stairway, past her bedroom and into his. She looked up at him, openly amused. "Rafe, your grandmother. What . . . ?"

He ushered her over to his bed and toppled her onto it with him, holding her above him. "I think she's very aware that humans are endowed with sexual drives." He dropped a kiss in the hollow of her breasts just where the neckline veed. "At least twice she's experienced that drive, I believe, producing my father and my uncle."

"But she was married, Rafe—something that you and I aren't."

And that little nagging part of her conscience reminded her of all the women he had had before her. A thousand of them, and she was but a thousand and one.

"The beauty and wonder of sex don't exist solely within the bounds of marriage, love. Oh, Mary, you excite me so much."

She loved the way he kissed her so intensely. His kisses made love to her lips, her throat, the undersides of her arms, even her hair. Wanting access to all of her, he rolled her beneath him. Her eyes closed, she drifted in abandon beneath the stroking of his hands until he grunted, "These damned panty hose!"

She gurgled with laughter and scrambled from his hold to stand at the foot of the bed. His eyes were ablaze with excitement as he lay, arms crossed behind his head, and watched her strip the panty hose from her legs. She could feel the excitement growing in her also as she unzipped the dress and dropped it over her hips. If only she could sustain her excitement, if only fear did not come between her and Rafe.

She stood before him clad only in her black lacy bikinis and bra. The narrowed slits of his eyes contained the fierce fire burning behind the pupils, and she was both thrilled and afraid of the sensual intensity and power of this man. Her hands rose with uncertainty to cross before her near-naked breasts.

"Mary," he groaned softly. "Just looking at you makes my mouth dry as a desert dune." He uncoiled and rolled from the bed. "Let me finish for you."

Speech was not in her power at that moment.

His large hands, strong and capable and callused, slid around her rib cage to deftly unhook the bra, his lips trailing tiny kisses along her shoulder in the process. Then she was unbound. Her eyes closed at his fingers' feverish touch on her breast, and she shivered uncontrollably, then tensed when he stepped back to behold her.

"Don't," he commanded. "Look at me, Mary. I don't want you to be afraid. I want you to enjoy what happens between us."

Reluctantly she opened her eyes to see the pleading that tempered the hungry desire etched in his face.

"Say the words, Mary—say that you want me." His hands slid to her waist, anchoring her roughly against him. "Say my name. I want to hear it on your lips!"

Her lips seemed stiff, the words coming hesitantly. "I want you, Rafe." And she realized then that she did, heaven help her.

Slowly, as though relishing the work, he slid the tiny bikini down over her hips. She was surprised and thrilled to feel his hands tremble with his intense excitement. His fingers caressed the backs of her knees, and she clutched at his shoulders to keep from buckling with the sheer pleasure of his touch. When his mouth lightly tasted the skin at the fork of her thighs she gave a soft little cry.

"Mary, honey," he whispered, "you're so fragrant there."

What he was doing was for her both an exquisite torment and terribly embarrassing. Her hands fluttered to her face, and he rose, standing before her, waiting. A long moment passed with both of them reaching a decision. He, to allow her to control what was to happen; she, to cast off her inhibitions and enjoy the intoxicating experience to its fullest.

Her hands dropped from her face to touch the narrow ruffles of his starched linen shirt. One by one she unfastened the buttons within the ruffles' folds, her fingers fumbling nervously. She spread the shirt's lapels wide to reveal the hard small nipples nested in the mat of tufted, wiry hair. Her teeth nipped softly at one flat nipple, and she was rewarded by his sharply indrawn breath.

Yet he made no move to touch her. Emboldened by her success, she continued her concentrated quest, but her teeth nibbled at her lower lip, betraying her trepidation. Yet to be completely in charge—it gave her a heady sense of power. She dropped to her knees to lower the trousers' zipper with a tantalizing slowness that was not premeditated. The exposed blue briefs could not contain his urgency. Forgetting her anxiety, she moved her body into his, her head pressed against him.

"Mary . . . Mary . . . you're a devil woman." He whispered her name over and over. His body was taut with raw hunger.

"Rafe . . .," Her finger touched him, then caressed him. "Your body is beautiful!" she said, her voice filled with wonder.

With a harsh gasp he drew her to her feet, and she could no longer keep his hands at bay. Her head lolled back, offering her creamy throat to his devouring kisses.

After a moment she drew away, her independent will afraid of total capitulation. She smiled almost shyly at the hunger in his face. The fine tension that sang between them was intoxicating, like fizzy champagne. Her hands cupped his face, and she kissed him softly, almost fearfully, her tongue playing along his lips, her breasts brushing his chest.

He groaned. "You're driving me to the point of explosion, Mary!"

He let her go no further, but took control of the pace of their lovemaking by scooping her in his arms and moving back to the bed with her. His fingers scattered the pins in her hair, and the russet mane fluttered over the bedcovers. As he crouched above her, his hot golden-brown eyes scorched her skin. His head dipped and his tongue left its moist mark in her navel.

"Rafe, show me what to do," she whispered, feeling the urgency being kindled somewhere deep within her by the hands that electrified her with excitement, that same need she had known in those last explosive moments in the shower with him. She glorified in the hot awareness of being totally feminine, and her arms reached out in surrender to this man who had pursued her so relentlessly.

When he slipped inside her there was that cautious tightening, the friction of pain. He halted, enfolded just within her. He seemed so large, she was afraid she couldn't contain him. His hands caressed her hair, his palms damp now with raw excitement and the agony of apprehension.

"It's all right, Mary, love. We have all the time in the world."

She realized that his control was severely strained

and lay absolutely still when he resumed stroking with small, hesitant moves until he was fully inside her. Then she forgot all in the awesomeness of his powerful lovemaking.

"Rafe," she whispered softly, "I didn't know. I didn't know."

He was inside her. Deep, and pressing deeper. Her muscles squeezed in satiny response to his quickened stroking. He kissed her wildly, hotly, mouthing his words of intense passion against her parted lips. "Oh, honey, Mary, are you ready for me?" he gasped thickly. "I can't hold off much longer!"

She knew he wanted desperately to please her. And he was—he was loving all of her senses. She was floating outside of herself. What was happening to her was stunning, richly erotic. She had entered a sensual paradise she had not known existed. Her hands gripped his back, feeling the muscles flex beneath her palms, as she joined him in the wild ride, slamming against him, taking him deeper within her. She writhed under him, her hips rotating with his plunging, her lips moaning in ecstatic abandon.

Then she was going over the edge.

And her startled cries, her body's convulsive reaction, drove him over the edge with her.

Chapter 13

A THIN BLUE PLUME OF CIGARETTE SMOKE CORKSCREWED into the air. Languorously Mary watched it dissipate. She was trying to sort out her feelings. Perhaps she should be feeling shame, but there had been no promiscuity, no indiscriminate sex involved. Only wildly beautiful lovemaking.

She also knew that there would never be another man in her life. Not even Rafe. There was only this one moment in time for the two of them.

"Rafe?"

"Hmmm?"

Almost shyly she entwined her fingers in the mat of curls on his bronzed chest. "What are you thinking?"

He ground out the cigarette in the ashtray at the side of the bed and turned to her. He studied her upturned face for a long moment before he spoke. The almost physical possession of his gaze sent her pulse pounding in her eardrums all over again. Absently his fingers ensnared the silken hair that curled about her shoulders. "I'm thinking that your luscious little rear feels as luscious as it looks, that—"

"You were not!" she laughed softly.

"All right." His voice grew serious. "You rarely talk about your past. I was thinking I'd like to know more about you. A whole lot more, honey. Everything."

"Like what?" she asked cautiously.

"Oh, why you've never married."

She stiffened. The past was a difficult subject for her to discuss, especially after the intimacy of lovemaking. But she sensed that he would not let her evade his question. "Partially because I didn't have the time to ever become involved with anyone. I was too busy trying to make something of my life. There were brothers and sisters to see to, school to get through. And I knew that getting married, having a baby—I might sink back into the life I had known as a child."

He was relentless. "What kind of life was that?"

Her voice was dry, unemotional. It was the only sane way she could talk about the past. "Dehumanizing poverty."

"Go on," he prompted, but with infinite gentleness.

"I . . . I didn't want to see my children born with shortened life spans because of improper nourishment

—or farmed out to other homes because of my inability to care for them. I'm the eldest of nine children, Rafe."

Her voice dropped to a mere whisper. "Most of the others died early in life, or were separated from me by adoption. One was severely retarded because my mother lacked adequate care during pregnancy. Another is in prison. With my father wandering the land most of the time, and my mother unable to cope . . ."

She shrugged, but she could feel that she was dangerously close to losing control. "I tried hard to keep the family together. There are only two left now besides myself—Billy, of course, and a sister, Amy."

"That's why you specialized in maternal and infant care," he mused gently.

She turned her head into the pillow created by his chest and arm, loving the delicious smell of him. She didn't really want to talk anymore. "It's my way of establishing my own family unit, I suppose," she said on a final note, hoping the discussion was over.

He propped himself on one elbow and stared intently at her face. "And your virginity?" His voice was full of wonder. "Why did you wait so long to give it? It certainly wasn't because you were frigid, I can assure you of that."

A wry smile curved her lips. She traced the long, drooping lines of his mustache with her fingertip. "Like I told you, I was so busy, so driven to make something of my life—to become a doctor—that I honestly never had time for dates, for men. After a while I just assumed that I had no sexuality. Like a table." She dimpled. "Until I met Rafe Anaya."

He bent and brushed his lips against hers. "Mary?" he murmured against her mouth.

"Hmmm?"

"Nothing. Just thank you for tonight."

She knew that soon the respite would be over, that she would return to her spinster's world. Her arms wrapped around him. He kissed her vividly flushed face. And even as those kisses changed, he was inevitably rolling over atop her, filling his hands with her buttocks. Once again that rich, hot coil of excitement spiraled through her. She wanted him between her legs. She kissed his beard-shadowed jaw, his ears, his nose, his mouth, his hard-ridged shoulders. Hot little kisses that said she wanted to crawl inside him. She savored his hot naked flesh against her own.

He lay between her thighs while he suckled her sweet breasts, swirling her pouting nipples with his tongue. There was just the hint of savage, restrained hunger in those kisses. After a while his breath began to come in short, hot bursts. He slipped up slightly, pausing to insinuate himself just inside her, and she gasped with the intensity of the pleasure.

"Mary, honey, you like what I'm doing, don't you?"

"Oh, yes, Rafe. Love me. Love me."

He moved up astride her then. He felt astoundingly good between her legs, and, shockingly, she was spreading them achingly to take in more. Her body flowed back into his again and there was nothing but the two of them united in the wild, mindless ecstasy.

"So good, so good," he said thickly against her pillow of curls.

When her hands clenched against his back and she thought she was going to shatter into a thousand pieces, he slowed the pace to a rich, euphoric lovemaking, lying within her—absolutely still—for a few moments. But she could feel him throbbing within her and wanted to beg him to continue, to end this pain/pleasure. But his quiet, tender kisses urged her to trust him, to follow his lead.

He taught her what he liked, how to please him, and in turn discovered the touches and kisses that aroused her. On and on they went until they satisfied one another in a curiously sweet—but nonetheless powerful—climax.

Afterward she lay in his arms, tucked into him, fitting him perfectly. Just when she thought his breathing was steady and even with sleep, he said, "Mary, if you awaken before I do, don't touch me to wake me up. Just slide over to your side of the bed and say something. Quietly."

"Why?" she asked, puzzled at the request.

"Left over from the war—Nam," was his simple

reply. "I sometimes lash out without realizing where I am."

Of course, she should have known. A part of her ached to reach out and comfort him. But she understood why he wouldn't let anyone get that close. If there were enough time remaining for the two of them, perhaps . . .

Perhaps it was better that there wasn't.

Mary grated the cheese over the sliced potatoes. Beside her Ysabel Anaya's veined hands deftly diced the onions. Forgetting herself, Mary hummed a little tune. She hadn't known many Thanksgiving dinners. From the living room came the excited sound of the football commentator. Last time she had peeked, Rafe was stretched out on the couch asleep. So the arduous night had left its mark on him, also.

"My dear," Ysabel said, "you can't imagine what pleasure having the two of you here has brought me. For so long now I've despaired of Rafe settling down."

"I don't think he's quite ready," Mary said cautiously.

"Of course he isn't." Ysabel turned the onions into the casserole dish. "All his life he's been shuffled from one house to another, one apartment to another, one country to another. That was why he joined the Special Forces. Always on the move—it was all he had ever known. It took something awfully traumatic—I don't know what it was—to make him settle down in one place, to come back to Kingdom Come. It'll take something equally traumatic to make him settle down with one woman."

During Thanksgiving dinner Rafe watched Mary, sitting across the long dining table from him. With his grandmother between them, it was agony not to reach out and touch her. He felt vividly alive, attuned to every movement in the earth's makeup, attuned wholly to Mary Margulies. He was truly astonished by his continued wanting of her and how richly she satisfied him. He was going to keep her with him until the day he tired of her. Somehow he would convince her to stay.

She had tartly lectured him about his excesses and the lateness of the night, and then surprised him—and herself—by making love to him, riding astride him this time, her hair falling over his chest and face as she took them to a pulse-pounding, stunning flood of release.

He had thought, with each coupling, that the wanting of her would diminish. But it hadn't. To his surprise, his desire for her only burned that much more fiercely, like an uncontrollable prairie wildfire. What had happened to his presumptuous opinion that lovemaking was only his due after an evening spent with a woman, happily accepted and quickly forgotten?

He had thought—no, hoped—that after this weekend he would be in command of his life again. But such evidently would not be the case. Just sitting there across from Mary, he could feel the need rising to be one with her again. And again. No other woman had ever pleased him so. But what worried him was that this feisty little thing brooked no interference in her career and its future.

Her pink tongue stole out to wipe a drop of salad dressing from her lips, and he came completely undone. He had to get her home to his house, quickly, where they could be totally alone and he could make love to her until he died of exhaustion.

He laid his napkin beside his plate. "Marvelous dinner, Grandmother. Just great. But it's late, and Mary has to get back to her practice tomorrow."

"Rafe!" Mary exclaimed in a startled voice. "The dessert hasn't even been served yet!"

His grandmother swallowed her tea with choked laughter. "Oh, Mary! You're enchanting, my child, positively enchanting! And you, Rafe, haven't changed a bit."

"Oh, but I have, Grandmother," he said in a solemn tone. "I have."

The old lady kept a discreet but avid eye on her grandson as he proceeded to get himself under control and finish his meal. She wanted great-grandchildren. But a granddaughter-in-law first. She had just about given up hope. Rafe was on his way to being a dyed-in-the-wool bachelor. Unless this very lovely, very sweet and very intelligent young lady could convince him otherwise.

But what if Mary Margulies had no interest in taming her wild grandson? "You must come back and visit me often, Mary, dear. Without my grandson. He wouldn't understand women's talk."

The two women exchanged a wink of perfect communication.

Something nagged at the corner of Rafe's brain on the drive back to Kingdom Come. His feathers were slightly ruffled, and the hell of it was that he couldn't quite pinpoint why. He lit a cigarette and flicked a gaze at Mary, who sat silently watching the fields and mountains speed past. They were both exhausted by their nonstop lovemaking of the night before. He tossed the half-smoked cigarette out the window, put off by its stale taste.

The stale taste . . . Then he knew what was bothering him. The old thrill of selecting a woman for the evening and the ensuing challenge of seduction and eventually victory had left only a stale taste in his mouth lately.

By damn, he was hopelessly in love enough to want Mary forever! Forever. Forever was enough to frighten him . . . but not if he had Mary in his arms . . . forever.

Darkness was settling over the community of Kingdom Come when he parked the MG before his house. "Aren't you going to take me home, Rafe?"

"No." He put his arms around her and held her tightly to him, grinning down at her.

Instantly she was suspicious. "Let me go." She squirmed. "And take me home this instant."

"No."

She began playfully fighting him, pushing at his hands, and the more she pushed, the more he laughed. Her carefully arranged hair came undone, and her breasts bobbled against his chest, inciting him now to pure lust. She saw it in his eyes. She knew it was coming, and she couldn't help herself. She wanted him.

She made one last effort. "You take me home right now, Rafe Anaya," she ground out in a stern voice, "or I'll walk home on my own!"

"Just try it!" he roared. But he was laughing.

It became a contest for her to resist him, for him to conquer her. Her body trembled with blazing excitement as his hands grappled with her flailing ones. Somehow in the confines of that small car he pinned her half beneath him and half against the door and opened her blouse. His hand delved into her bra and freed one breast. His breath was hot and seared her flesh.

Suddenly, shakily, he drew away.

Confused, she tried to control her rapid breathing. "What is it, Rafe?"

Without releasing her he began to talk, quietly, carefully, as if feeling his way over uncharted ground. "Honey, I love you, and I want you to stay in Kingdom Come. I want you to marry me."

He had said he loved her! Yet her lips mumbled, "No."

"In the name of all the saints, why not?"

"Will you leave Rancho Encantado and your people and this valley to move with me to Washington?"

He shifted uncomfortably. "Isn't Kingdom Come a good enough place to practice?"

"Practice?" She tried to lower her voice, which had crescendoed shrilly. "You yourself warned me that no one would accept an outsider, a spinster! I have no practice in Kingdom Come and never will!"

"That answer won't satisfy me. Do you think I'd give up so easily? I've never wanted anything in my life like I want you." He gave a dry, mocking laugh. "Hell, I've never had to work for anything in my life like I've had to work for you. I should have given up after the first month, but my male pride was piqued."

She heard the acrid self-loathing in his voice, but she couldn't help her tart reply. "And that's all it is, Rafe. Male pride. If I acquiesced now you would be having second thoughts within another month."

"Try me?" In the dark she sensed more than saw his bitter smile.

But she couldn't respond in a light fashion. "Rafe, don't make it hard for me, please."

"And don't make me grovel, Mary. For God's sake, I want to marry you!"

She tried for a light touch. Anything to avoid the wrenching emotional scene that was coming. "Let me up, you oaf. You're heavy!"

For once he complied, almost savagely jerking her to a sitting position. Abruptly his hands released her shoulders. "A prestigious career means more to you than love," he ground out in terse, tight words, not disguising the loathing in his voice. "In my books that doesn't make you much of a woman, much less a person."

His words stung because they struck at her vulnerable conscience, this child of the streets, this flare child. "How can you set yourself up to judge me! You've had everything you ever wanted. How can you understand what it's like to be poor, to walk the streets at four in the morning because there's no place to go but back to a cramped derelict car? How would you know what it feels like for the welfare department to carry away the only things you've ever loved—your brother, and then a sister and another sister?"

Her hands were clenched, and her jaws hurt because she was gritting her teeth so tightly. "I've worked too long, too hard, to jeopardize a brilliant career by burying myself in a desert wilderness."

He started up the car. "Then go bury yourself with your precious plants. That's all they're good for—substitute love for a substitute woman!"

She put out her hand. "Rafe, please, try to understand."

"I do, Mary. I've been a fool. There are other honey pots that I can dip into, much sweeter-tasting than what I've been wasting my time on. Women who are real flesh and blood, not computer-charted careers."

It had been another fruitless day at the clinic. Mary parked her car beneath the spreading lime trees and listlessly made her way to the adobe. Then a "Pssst! Psssst!" halted her plodding footsteps.

She glanced up to see a woman standing in the shadow of the yard's mimosa. "Who is it?"

"Angelita Vargas," the woman said, stepping forward to expose her ample girth.

Mary crossed to her. "Is something wrong? Has something happened to Tranquilito, Angelita?"

The woman ducked her head, tripling her chins. "No. No. I come here instead of the clinic so my husband would not know where I was."

Mary took the woman's dimpled elbow. "Come on inside for some lemonade, Angelita, and you can tell me all about your problem."

"No, *soltera*. I have deep shame."

"Tell me what troubles you, Angelita."

In the dry heat of the afternoon the woman proceeded to tell Mary of what had transpired since her previous visit. "So you see, *soltera,* when my husband found out I had gone to you, he was *muy enojado,* very angry with me! Later that night Fernando went down to your office. It was he who"—her plump hands searched for the English words—"who messed it up."

So the mystery of the ransacked office was solved. "Thank you for coming to me, Angelita."

Hesitantly the woman held forth three crisp five-dollar bills. "I know this will not pay for all the mess, but it is all I have been able to save in so short a time."

Mary started to gently push the hand away, to tell the woman that the cost was of no consequence. But she knew that the woman's honor, her great Hispanic pride, was at stake. "Thank you, Angelita. This will greatly help in replacing the medicines that were destroyed."

The woman's grin stretched from ear to ear. She had no more to say and was about to leave. "Angelita, how is Tranquilito doing with his problem? His bed-wetting?"

The toe of the woman's huarache dug into the sparse grass. "It is the same, *soltera*. Fernando, he will not let Tranquilito wash the sheets. It is a woman's job."

The old Latin *machismo*. "And the salt intake I prescribed?"

"Fernando says that if *la curandera* finds out I went to you, she will—"

Mary held up a hand. "I know. She will never treat your family again."

"*Sí, soltera.*"

With a dejected sigh Mary watched Angelita lumber away. Her work at Kingdom Come seemed so hopeless, and she wondered why she even bothered to try to reach out to the *barrio* people. Perhaps it was because their rejection stung her professional pride.

She could hold out for the remainder of her tenure at Kingdom Come. If only she didn't have to run into Rafe on the streets so often. The contempt in his eyes would have wilted even her plants.

Chapter 14

RAFE GLARED AT THE TELEPHONE LIKE IT WAS A RATTLER. He was sorely tempted. His fingers drummed on the side of the beer can.

Eddie walked into the den with two more cans of beer. "Go ahead. Call her."

"Call who?" Rafe asked innocently.

"Who?" Eddie hooted. He passed a can to Rafe, then settled his lanky length in the leather chair across from the sofa and propped his boots on the coffee table. "The pretty little woman who was at the Oasis with Brewster last night, that's who."

A black scowl lowered Rafe's brows. "The low-down weasel, poaching on a staked-out claim."

"Man, you act like you're in the last stage of disintegration."

Rafe eyed his friend sourly. "She wants a career

more than she wants a man. And now she's leaving at the end of the month."

"Convince her that you're worth a career. Let her know you're serious. Tell her that you want to marry her."

"I did."

Eddie spewed the beer across his upraised legs. "You did? By damn! You do have it bad. Maybe you should see a doctor."

"I am. I was."

Eddie gazed at his friend with humorous concern. "I must say, ol' friend, you had this coming."

"Thanks, ol' friend." Rafe downed the newest can of beer in eleven seconds flat and crushed the can between his fingers. "Now what the hell can I do about it?" he muttered gloomily.

"Got just the cure. What say we cruise over to Juárez and tie one on at Papa Gallego's? They say there's a new piece of pretty fluff there."

Rafe considered the suggestion for a serious thirty seconds. He hadn't really wanted another woman since he opened the closet door to fix the water heater and Mary's luscious body and crazy vivacity hit him between the eyes. "Naw. I want Mary. But she isn't worth the effort."

He was heartily sick of the whole mess. He lurched to his feet and ambled out of the den toward the kitchen and another beer. He was possessed by the deliberate intention to drink himself into a hilarious and glorious exultation. "Maybe I just oughtta become a monk."

"Don't think Father John would approve of that," Eddie observed with another tilt of his can. "Nor half the female population of Kingdom Come."

"It's not half the female population I want," Rafe growled, noting that the refrigerator shelves were empty of beer. He felt like crying. It was because he was out of beer, he told himself.

The letterhead was elegantly scripted with the words "Scott-Waggoner Medical Complex, Ltd." The letter was signed by the director of recruiting.

The board of directors of the Medical Complex has instructed me to inform you of their unanimous decision to accept you for a position on the staff. We feel you will be an asset to Scott-Waggoner and look forward to our association and the opportunity of working with you.

How long she had been waiting to read those words! Years. Since as long ago, really, as the week she had spent in the county hospital as a child with scarlet fever.

The rest of the letter dealt with the day her employment would commence—January 3 of the coming year; the terms of employment; and the initial salary —an astronomical figure, in her mind. As instructed, she executed the enclosed employment agreement and set out for the post office, Vicente's *tienda*. She was in haste to return the contract immediately. After it was mailed there could be no turning back. Her decision would be irrevocably made.

An end had come to the interminable sunshine of

the desert autumn. An arctic storm front had bulged down out of Canada that first week in December. So much for Rafe's Chamber of Commerce speech about year-round sunshine, Mary thought drearily, and hugged her beige wool coat tighter about her as she made her way the short distance from the car to the *tienda*. The cold wind practically shoved her through the door.

"Hola, soltera," Vicente called from behind the checkout counter. It was a jovial greeting, but she thought that uneasiness lurked in his soft black eyes.

"Hello, Vicente. How's it—?"

She broke off as Rafe rounded the corner of an aisle, striding toward the counter. She had seen him several times since the disastrous Thanksgiving weekend, but never at so close a distance that the formalities of civilized speech were exchanged. She had forgotten how catastrophic a look from those brown eyes could be. No, she really hadn't, but she had tried to make herself forget. In that sheepskin jacket with its collar turned up he looked like he had stepped out of the pages of one of those classy male magazines. Gorgeous.

Beneath that hot gaze she wanted to run, she wanted to melt. Surely she could handle this uncomfortable situation in a mature, adult manner.

He set a box of green tea—and another of antacids—on the counter. "Well, hel-lo, Mary."

The greeting was easy, and she followed his lead. Best to end their relationship on amicable terms. She smiled and managed to say just as easily, "Hello, Rafe."

She handed Vicente the letter with its Scott-Waggoner address and said, "Will you mail this for me?"

"So you've finally been accepted?" Rafe asked, his expression bland.

"Yes, finally." She eyed the bottle of antacids. "Heartburn?"

Above the stringently set lips his mustache quirked. "I think it's the green tea."

Vicente stood between them, watching the exchange with worried eyes that said the whole world had gone mad.

"Why don't you give up the tea?"

Rafe braced his hands on the counter and grimaced. "I can't. I'm hooked."

"Well, good-bye."

"So long, Mary."

A completely senseless, inane conversation, she thought dismally on the drive back home. Everything that could be said already had been.

Several times that week she reread the Scott-Waggoner letter—out of disbelief that after all those years of struggling just to make it through high school, then college, and finally med school, she had finally achieved her goal: to practice medicine in an influential, prestigious clinic.

With each reading she was more convinced than ever that she was doing the right thing in leaving

Kingdom Come. Good sense and logic pointed to the fact that she was almost useless here as a physician. Next time, the Mission Outreach Services could apply for a physician who was a married male, preferably a Hispanic. Certainly such a physician could better serve the community.

La Jean stuck her head inside the office door. "Manuel Ortega is here."

Mary's brows knitted. "Manuel Ortega? Is he a new patient?"

"We don't have a file on him. But he says it's important he sees you."

Mary rose and came around from behind her desk to step out into the reception office. As soon as she saw Manuel, she remembered him. Rafe's foreman. He was standing, and she noticed that he was coatless. He turned his sombrero between nervous hands. A furtive expression twitched in his eyes.

A sudden fear spiraled through her. "Has something happened to Rafe?"

"No, *soltera*. I cannot find *el patrón*. It is Hermalinda Hernández." He ducked his head. "It is her time, I think."

"Where is she?"

"I find the woman in the *bosque*—the trees where Rancho Encantado backs to the Rio Bravo. She tells me to bring *la soltera—pronto*."

Damn. Hermalinda was three weeks early. Mary took a deep breath. "Manuel, Josefita is a *partera*—a very good midwife. She can help deliver Hermalinda's baby."

He shook his head. "No. Hermalinda—she insists that you come. Come quickly. She says *gemelos*—twins—they give great pain. They won't come."

"You don't understand. I can't. It's against the law for me to help her. My license. I could lose it!"

But the wiry Mexican foreman just stood there. He understood nothing but the urgency of the moment.

Mary rubbed her sweaty palms together. She knew that this was what Hanson had been waiting for. If he caught her delivering Hermalinda's babies . . .

Yet there was that ache that had been growing in Mary all those years, what Aeschylus called "the pain that never sleeps," an ache for the flare children everywhere.

"La Jean," she said, totally in charge now, all indecisiveness vanquished, "get my bag. Manuel, we'll take my car."

A big grin brightened his swarthy face. *"Sí, soltera."*

La Jean chomped anxiously on her gum. "Are you certain you want to do this, Mary?"

The corners of Mary's mouth rose in a self-derisive grin as she took the bag La Jean reluctantly handed her. "I'm certain that I must be a very big fool."

Outside, the cold dry wind slammed against her, but she had been in too big a hurry to get her coat. Since Manuel knew exactly where to go, she let him drive. The Mustang bumped and careened over the rugged dirt road that snaked across Rancho Encantado land toward the Rio Grande's banks. The road dwindled to more of a cow trail, winding in and out of the prickly chaparral. Both she and Manuel kept scanning the horizon, checking for the dreaded sight of a green four-wheeler.

During the jolting trip Mary tried to reassure herself about Hermalinda. There was really no reason to worry. Except that Hermalinda was not the sort to complain of pain. Mary was willing to bet that the Indian woman had waited until the last moment to cross the river so that she could not be turned back across the border. But from the river she would have come immediately to the clinic, unless she was unable.

Suddenly Mary remembered that Hermalinda must have waded across the river. Sick inside, Mary thought about how icy cold the water had to be and knew that there could be other complications to worry about—including hypothermia. Why hadn't she thought to bring blankets?

"Hurry, Manuel!" Mary urged, and the man floored the accelerator like a berserk New York City taxi driver. A mesquite nearly missed losing its life.

Manuel glanced in the rearview mirror. "Uh-oh!"

"What is it?" Mary turned to look behind.

A cloud of dust sprayed upward like a rooster's tail from another vehicle trailing them. The race was on. Her stomach contracted in sudden ulceric pains.

Ahead, in the near distance, towered the bare branches of the spindly desert willows, scrub oaks and cottonwoods that marked the river's course. Manuel slowed the Mustang, his head poking in one direction, then another, looking.

"Well?" Mary asked anxiously. Despite the cold, perspiration beaded her upper lip. She might have been the woman in labor, for all her body's signs.

Manuel's face furrowed. "I can't remember exactly where I leave the woman, *soltera.*"

Mary's freckles blanched. "Son of a—"

"No—look! There, *soltera!*" Manuel's dirt-stained finger pointed toward clumps of high winter grass that banded a large cottonwood. "I left her there."

The little Mustang spun to a halt at the foot of the bank, and Mary was out and sprinting up the slope with her bag. Shielded by the high grass, Hermalinda lay propped against the cottonwood's trunk. She was nude from the waist up, with only Manuel's jacket spread over her upper torso to give her some protection—inadequate though it was—against the cold.

Apparently, after she had waded across the river, labor contractions had prevented her from finishing dressing. A plaid blouse and one huarache poked from the plastic garbage bag at her side. Her lids were squeezed shut, and her olive complexion was blanched as white as the dust trail that had pursued the Mustang.

Mary knelt beside her, and the young girl opened her eyes and raised her head. Sweat drenched her brow, and she was panting with the force of her contractions. Her body was shivering intensely with the cold.

"I could walk no farther. The pain. But the babies —they will not come."

Mary relaxed, but only slightly. The girl's skin color wasn't too good, but she seemed to have little problem with coordination or difficulty in talking. Warm blankets—if she could get them—would forestall hypothermia. She pushed the girl's dirt-stained skirt up over her thighs, and Manuel turned his back.

"The auto—it comes nearer," he warned.

Gently Mary performed a quick examination. Her mouth moved in what seemed a hopeless prayer: that the approaching vehicle wasn't Hanson; that the examination would reveal that labor was progressing normally.

The first prayer was answered with Manuel's relieved shout, "It's *el patrón*'s pickup!"

Mary breathed another silent prayer—this one of thanks—and steadily continued her examination. But she already knew the prognosis when her hand encountered the buttocks of the lower twin. And Hermalinda's pelvis was not of adequate size!

With a worried grimace she drew the skirt down over Hermalinda's thighs and rose just as Rafe loped up the bank. A swath of honey-brown hair tumbled over his forehead, and dirt streaked one high cheekbone.

"I saw your car go by," he said. His gaze swept the scene before him. "Trouble?"

"Breech birth, Rafe!" Mary was shivering so badly that she couldn't have performed surgery. "We need to get her back to the clinic. Immediately!"

Rafe jerked off his sheepskin jacket and threw it around Mary's shoulders. "We'll put the girl in the back of the pickup." He knelt and scooped up the heavy pregnant girl in his arms with a grunt of exertion. The muscles in his neck and forearms strained with his effort to walk without jarring his burden.

"I shouldn't have eaten so much, no?" Hermalinda joked, but another spasm of pain crossed her square-set face and twisted her lips.

"I'll get in the back with her," Mary said. But after Rafe gingerly lowered Hermalinda into the pickup's bed he turned to Mary and caught her shoulders. She wanted to slump against his chest, but he held her away from him, his gaze at once curious and piercing. "You know what you're doing, Mary—the repercussions if you're caught?"

She nodded wearily. "Don't tempt me to refuse to help her now."

While Rafe drove, Mary and Manuel sat with Hermalinda, cradling her body with theirs to soften the jolts. Fortunately there was a horse blanket there and, smelly though it was, it served to ward off what felt like subzero wind.

It seemed an eternity before the cinder-block clinic came into view. La Jean already had the door open for Rafe. Mary ran ahead of him to begin preparations.

Protecting the woman he carried, he shouldered his way inside and strode toward the first examination room. Mary was already there, washing her hands and arms with an antiseptic soap.

Her hands trembled visibly as she searched through the trays and gathered the necessary surgical instruments. She knew that with modern surgical tech-

niques there was little risk to the mother and child—if
the cesarean section could be performed in time. But
she was also very much aware that she was performing
an emergency procedure under less-than-ideal conditions.

Behind her Rafe gently edged Hermalinda onto the
examination table.

La Jean and Manuel stood at the door, both looking
very pale. "I'll . . . I'll wait out here," La Jean said.

Mary nodded absently. "Anchor her feet in the
stirrups," she instructed Rafe over her shoulder as
she crossed to the sink. Rapidly she scrubbed down
again. There was no cap, gown, or mask to worry
with; neither was there time.

She flicked a glance at Rafe. "You aren't faint-
hearted, are you?"

Beneath his mustache his lips curled in a rueful
smile. "After dealing with you, I suppose I can handle
anything."

"I'm going to administer a local anesthetic. It may
not be effective enough. Can you hold her if she
should move suddenly?"

"I can."

Hermalinda gasped between clenched teeth, "I will
not move."

But Hermalinda couldn't know the enormity of
what her body would undergo.

Mary draped a sheet over Hermalinda's upper
torso, then thoroughly scrubbed the woman's abdomen with an antiseptic. Finally she administered the
anesthetic. Hermalinda never winced.

Waiting for the anesthetic to take effect, Mary laid out the surgical instruments in the order she would need them. Her hands no longer trembled. She was in her element, entirely certain of her capabilities, her skills and her training. But time was working against her.

She tested the area to be incised for numbness and was satisfied. "We're ready," she told Rafe.

He nodded. Perspiration sheened his face now.

Once started, the operation wouldn't take long. She began, glancing only once at Hermalinda. The girl's stubby-nailed hands clutched at the table's metal bars. Her face was strained into a death mask, but she managed a grimace of encouragement. "You must give my children their gift of citizenship, *soltera.*"

Mary nodded with a reassuring smile she did not feel and briskly proceeded with her task.

A commotion at the doorway caught her peripheral attention, but she went back to the delicate, intricate work—until Hanson's hulk loomed over her, casting a shadow across the sheet covering the patient.

"I'm taking you in, Dr. Margulies." His gravelly voice was gloating. "As a public servant of the U.S. government, you are violating the law by administering to an illegal alien."

She swallowed the lump that threatened to seal off her throat and spared the man a glance. His sunglasses reflected the overhead surgical light, seeming to blind her. His smile was mean. "Let's go, Doc."

He took her arm, only to drop it immediately as his body was slammed against the wall. Rafe held him at the neck by his tie. The two were of equal height, though Hanson was stockier. At once she went back to work, but she could hear Rafe's voice, low and measured. "You aren't taking the doctor anywhere yet, Hanson. You're going to wait right here until she finishes the operation, all right?"

No answer came, but the Border Patrol agent must have nodded, for Rafe snapped, "Good!"

Undeterred by the interruption, she finished the incision with unshaken precision to encounter the infants nestled in the open womb. Carefully lifting one, she quickly cut the umbilical cord. With a howl from its gumless little O of a mouth, the baby—a wrinkled red girl—made her presence in the world known.

Mary laid the child in the crook of Hermalinda's arm. "An American citizen, Hermalinda—and another one is shortly on the way."

When Mary laid the second infant, a boy this time, into the snug hollow of Hermalinda's other arm, tears glistened in the girl's eyes. *"Gracias, soltera,"* the girl choked out. *"Mil gracias."*

"Happy birthday," Mary whispered to the squalling babies, and blinked back her own tears at the little miracle in which she had been permitted to play a part.

"Bravo!" Rafe commended her from behind, his voice husky with the importance of the moment.

"My babies," Hermalinda asked, "they are all right?"

"They're perfect, Hermalinda."

In back of her she heard Rafe growl, "Not yet, Hanson."

She called La Jean's name, and the woman poked her head in the door with obvious reluctance. Behind La Jean, Manuel was genuflecting. "Take the babies from Hermalinda," Mary instructed, "and clean them up."

La Jean's eyes seemed to expand, if it were possible for them to get any larger. "Me?"

"You can do it—there's nothing to it."

The rest was anticlimactic—the cleanup work, which involved removing the placentas, closing the abdominal wall with sutures and removing the splotches of blood from both Hermalinda and herself.

At last she faced Rafe and Hanson. "I'm ready."

The physical restraint Rafe had used on Hanson was made up for by the other man's unleashed anger. He grabbed her arm and shoved her ahead of him so that she stumbled against the medicine cabinet, catching her head on its sharp metal corner.

Rafe exploded then. Stunned by the blow she had taken, Mary watched in horrified silence as Rafe came at Hanson, who was so much beefier. But Rafe's hand sliced through the air like a bayonet, catching Hanson in the shoulder. The man staggered, but retaliated with a heavy punch that caught Rafe in the ribs. He seemed to double over, but when Hanson moved in, Rafe's leg lashed out so quickly that it was only a blurred movement, and Hanson toppled with a thud.

Mary had seen that kind of fighting only in programs dealing with the Far East. Quick and lethal martial arts.

At once Rafe was astride Hanson, beating him with malletlike fists. "Rafe!" she cried, afraid of the grimly violent intent she saw in his face. "You'll kill him! Stop!"

A small, wry smile poked at Mary's lips. Hermalinda had won the battle of wills; of the two of them, the Indian girl was the stronger after all.

Mary leaned her head back against the cinder-block wall of the cell in the city jail where she had been detained overnight, pending release on bail. Her skirt was rumpled from her sleepless night, and her blouse was splattered with bloodstains from the delivery.

There were only two cells on the jail's second floor—one for men and one for women. The only other occupant that morning was Willie the Wino, arrested on vagrancy. In that early hour of the morning he slept on his bunk in a peaceful afterhaze of intoxication.

However intent Hanson was in carrying out his duty and arresting her, he couldn't touch Rafe for obstructing justice. The *patrón* of the valley wielded far too much influence and had too many connections that stretched as far as El Paso and its more powerful law-enforcement agencies. Even Hanson recognized that, however much he resented it. And he did have her, which was what he had wanted all along.

In her lap was the morning's newspaper. Its headline shouted of her arrest, and the attendant column described the incident and its aftermath. The mother, Hermalinda Hernández, with her newborns, had been detained for several hours in El Paso, then hustled back across the border. Apparently Hermalinda had known what would happen all along. No authorities wanted to risk public wrath by incarcerating a mother nursing two infants.

But what would happen to Mary herself? Certainly when Scott-Waggoner learned of the scandal their offer would be withdrawn.

Desolate, she crumpled the newspaper between her hands.

Chapter 15

THE LAWYER FROM EL PASO WAS A BESPECTACLED middle-aged little man with thinning hair. He was dressed in a conservative three-piece suit. "Elmo McGruder of Brown, Harte and McGruder," he had introduced himself. Speaking with her on that initial visit in the cell, he had maintained a very professional manner. But she had not failed to see the curious speculation in his nondescript eyes—speculation combined with male appreciation.

On her part she had been surprised to learn that Rafe had hired a lawyer to represent her. Apparently what she had done—delivering Hermalinda's babies —had changed his mind about her. He had been there when she needed him. Hopefully he no longer loathed her. But did he still love her?

As he escorted Mary from the jail to his car,

McGruder explained her situation to her. "Actually, it would seem there is very little representing to be done in this case. You have become a *cause célèbre*. Since the news hit the national media yesterday an outpouring of sympathy for your plight has convinced the federal authorities in El Paso that this episode is best forgotten. Of course, there will be the obligatory hearing, but technically all charges have been dropped."

He opened the sleek black Mercedes' door for Mary, and she was glad for the car's warmth. The sun was shining, but the wind was raw with the latest blue norther.

McGruder came around the other side to slide behind the wheel. "You mean I'm free?" she asked, still not quite believing all that had happened in the past forty-eight hours. "I can still practice medicine?"

He smiled smugly. "Not only that, but the Border Patrol's regional commissioner is investigating the patrolman who arrested you. A Chief Hanson, I believe. It seems some citizens have volunteered information that doesn't shed a very favorable light on his career."

The mention of Hanson's career reminded her of her own. The dream of a career with Scott-Waggoner was little more than ashes now. As the lawyer drove away from the courthouse, she stared silently out the window. She was still so stunned by all that had happened that it was difficult for her to reassess her situation.

"Oh!" McGruder dug in his vest pocket with his

free hand and produced a yellow envelope. "This telegram arrived for you in care of the city jail."

He passed it to her and tactfully concentrated on the drive to her house while she tore open the envelope and read the contents. She felt delirious. Ecstatic. She wanted to shout. Scott-Waggoner wanted to commend her for her *humane action taken in the course of nearly insurmountable obstacles and reiterate that our staff looks forward to the addition of a doctor of your stature.*

From behind his horn-rimmed glasses McGruder's glance took in the desolate landscape, and his long, bony nose wrinkled in distaste. "Kingdom Come does look like the end of the world, doesn't it?" he asked rhetorically after she replaced the telegram in its envelope.

"I would have to agree." It was difficult to keep her tone as colorless as his when she felt so jubilant.

But the jubilation of the moment seemed to wane once she reached the adobe. She moved around the rooms in a kind of daze, toying with the potted plants, adjusting the slatted shutters, wiping a finger along the dusty coffee table, opening and closing the refrigerator. Food didn't appeal to her at the moment. She really didn't know what to do.

She really should begin packing.

She really should be celebrating.

She really felt like crying.

She really never had been practical or logical.

She took one last look at the telegram lying on the kitchen table and, turning on her heel, marched to the bedroom to pick up the telephone. "La Jean, I'm free. How soon can you come over to help me celebrate?"

The woman yelped and said she was on her way.

It was still too early in the morning for champagne —and, of course, Vicente's *tienda* didn't sell the bubbly stuff. But coffee with a friend with bright orange hair would do just as well.

A short while later a knock at the door produced La Jean, hands jammed in her denim pockets. Her smile flashed between snaps of her gum. "You can still practice medicine in Kingdom Come?"

Mary shut the door and started for the kitchen. "Only for my remaining three weeks."

La Jean trailed her. "You don't intend to stay?"

"That's another thing I'm celebrating, La Jean. Despite all the adverse publicity, I've been officially accepted by Scott-Waggoner Medical Complex in Washington. It's a real coup for a physician."

La Jean grabbed her and hugged her. "Gee, Mary, I'll hate to see you leave, but that's great!"

"How about some coffee to celebrate the occasion?"

"Got any tea?"

Mary grimaced. "I lost my taste for tea and threw all the tea bags out. Sorry."

She poured the coffee into two cups and settled herself at the table to enjoy some old-fashioned girl talk. La Jean related the excitement that had claimed the community since Mary's arrest. While La Jean talked it occurred to Mary how much she would miss the woman.

And Rafe.

"You'll stay for my wedding?" La Jean asked, finishing the last of the coffee.

"I wouldn't miss it for the world."

She got up to pour La Jean another cup of coffee when the heavy brass iron on the front door announced another visitor. La Jean said, "I'll get it for you."

A minute later Mary heard La Jean say, "Oh, my . . ."

At the exclamation Mary deserted the kitchen and went into the living room to see what was so disturbing. La Jean beckoned to her and stepped back from the open door. Her eyes were wide with astonishment and her mouth was a perfect O. "Mary, kid, will you look!"

Mary looked. Her eyes blinked.

The yard was filled with people. As she began to distinguish faces amid the blur of humans, she realized that these were the people from the *barrio!*

She saw Angelito and Tranquilito. The man with his arm about Angelita had to be Fernando, who had vandalized the clinic. She spotted Ofelia Ruiz with her daughter and the baby Pedro. From the sea of faces she picked out those with illnesses whom Josefita had taken her to see on her rounds. Incredibly, even Hermalinda was there, supported by those toward the front. Grinning widely, she held a bawling twin in each arm. However had she managed to slip across the Rio Grande with two babies? Well, the girl was resourceful.

Josefita, with Carmelita and Lucero on either side of her, stepped forward from the crowd. A respectful hush settled over the *barrio* people. *"Soltera,"* Josefita said, "we come to you with *vergüenza*—with shame."

Behind Josefita heads nodded solemnly. "We didn't give you a chance to help us," the *curandera* continued, her rheumy eyes glistening with a hint of tears. "Delivering the *gemelos* as you did—we know now we were wrong. We want to plead with you not to leave us."

Mary knew this was a difficult speech for the proud old woman to make. But Mary could see in the wrinkled face that the woman meant every word. She couldn't remember ever being so touched by a gesture as the one made by these people before her.

But on the kitchen table lay the Scott-Waggoner letter that represented the sum total of her life—her past, her present and her future.

The December sun sparkled on the whitewashed walls around the Santo Tomás mission. The norther had blown through El Paso to waste itself in the Mexico badlands.

Beneath the mission's arched entrance Father John stood. He scratched his jaw. His ruddy face mirrored his puzzlement. "This is a very strange request, my daughter. The Santo Tomás bells are never rung except on the Lord's day and other religious holidays."

"I know," Mary said patiently. "But this is to

commemorate a very special date, Father John. The day the *hidalgo*'s spinster daughter died."

The old padre shook his head in bewilderment. "I am aware of the legend, but it doesn't seem to me that any special date was assigned to the—"

Mary held her breath, waiting as the old padre paused, trying to assimilate her request.

Then Father John's face brightened. "Ahh, I am beginning to understand." Abstractedly his fingers stroked the golden cross suspended from the thin chain around his white Roman collar. "Let's see if I've got this right, my daughter. I am to have the bells rung, then place a call to Rafael and remind him of the legend."

"Yes—and tell him that Kingdom Come's spinster has decided not to leave."

Would he come? She didn't know. True, she didn't think he loathed her any longer. But did he love her? She had asked herself that question so many times lately. . . . The not knowing hurt her stomach so badly that no antacid tablet could relieve the pain. Even her heart hurt. She paced the chapel, her heels clicking against the adobe-tiled floor. In the chapel's dimness her white linen jacket and skirt stood out, a ghostly vision. Perhaps the wandering soul of a lady of another century. A spinster lady.

Surely half an hour had passed.

"Mary."

Was that his voice that sounded so much like a frog's croak?

She whirled, and his heart ceased to function, then caught up with itself in a furious pounding. How beautiful, how spirited, how dear she was! He was assailed by doubts, shaken by the knowledge that he might lose her forever, and Father John's phone call had only confused him more, something about the tale of the spinster and the bell's song and Mary. He didn't seem to be able to think clearly anymore when it came to Mary.

For the first time since those intermittent moments of agony in serving with the Special Forces he felt totally helpless. Love could do that to a person. It gave a person the power to hurt. And she had that power over him.

But it also gave a person the power to bestow great joy. And she had that power, also.

Keeping his eyes on her face, precious and taut with anxiety, he raced down the aisle toward her in three long strides and caught her to him, his arms tightening around her painfully. He wanted to taste the sweetness of her from the wild red curls to the wild red toenail polish.

Just thinking about her nubile body caused his own body to quicken. And just thinking that she might still give that most desirable little body—and the perfection of her love—to another man made him want to pulverize someone with his bare hands.

"Rafe," she whispered against his beseeching mouth, "I was so afraid you wouldn't come."

"Oh, Mary, love. Do you remember the nightmare I had the night I was ill?"

She nodded, not understanding where his words were leading, but she was ready to follow . . . anywhere.

"It was a horrible dream, Mary. Of an experience in Nam, of death . . . and destruction . . . and everything that had made me realize my need to return to the valley and settle down forever. And it took something just as horrible to make me forget my resolve never to fight again. Hanson's mistreatment of you."

With a shudder she recalled the murderous look she had seen in Rafe's eyes, what he had done to the man because of her. And she recalled Ysabel Anaya's words that it would take something like that.

"Dear God, but I love you so much, Mary. If it takes me following you to Washington, then—"

Joyously, lovingly, she touched his cheek. "Rafe, you've got to know that while being a doctor is everything to me—my past, present and future—my future would never be complete without you in it. And the people of Kingdom Come are part of you. Here is where I want to be. Here is my home. At last I have a home," she whispered, almost to herself.

He heard her breath catch as his mouth became preoccupied with her neck. Incredible how just a smile and a few soft words of love from this fragile person could shake him to the core of his masculinity. She was so vulnerable and yet so strong. And willful. Willful enough that she could still change her mind. He took her face between his hands. "Mary, love, I'm going to be an absolute basket case until you officially agree to marry me."

She tilted her head back so that she could look up into his face, and he saw the absolute joy radiating in her eyes. He felt the same way. Absolute joy. And absolute love. And absolute lust. Only for—and forever for—this one woman. How soon could he marry her and hustle her off to their bedroom?

Far above in the belfry, bells began singing, celebrating the union of the Spinster and the Bachelor. And, of course, another story has now been added to the legend, and when strangers pass through Kingdom Come the *hacienda* of Rancho Encantado is always pointed out, with accompanying whispers about its enchanted couple.

If you enjoyed this book...

Thrill to 4 more
Silhouette Intimate Moments
novels (a $9.00 value)—
ABSOLUTELY FREE!

If you want more passionate sensual romance, then Silhouette Intimate Moments novels are for you!

In every 256-page book, you'll find romance that's electrifying...involving... and intense. And now, these larger-than-life romances can come into your home every month!

4 FREE books as your introduction.

Act now and we'll send you four thrilling Silhouette Intimate Moments novels. They're our gift to introduce you to our convenient home subscription service. Every month, we'll send you four new Silhouette Intimate Moments books. Look them over for 15 days. If you keep them, pay just $9.00 for all four. Or return them at no charge.

We'll mail your books to you *as soon as they are published.* Plus, with every shipment, you'll receive the Silhouette Books Newsletter absolutely free. *And Silhouette Intimate Moments is delivered free.*

Mail the coupon today and start receiving Silhouette Intimate Moments. Romance novels for women...not girls.

Silhouette Intimate Moments

Silhouette Intimate Moments™
120 Brighton Road, P.O. Box 5020, Clifton, NJ 07015

☐ YES! Please send me FREE and without obligation, 4 exciting Silhouette Intimate Moments romance novels. Unless you hear from me after I receive my 4 FREE books, please send 4 new Silhouette Intimate Moments novels to preview each month. I understand that you will bill me $2.25 each for a total of $9.00—with no additional shipping, handling or other charges. **There is no minimum number of books to buy and I may cancel anytime I wish.** The first 4 books are mine to keep, even if I never take a single additional book.

☐ Mrs. ☐ Miss ☐ Ms. ☐ Mr.   BMML24

Name	(please print)	
Address		Apt. #
City	State	Zip
Area Code	Telephone Number	

Signature (if under 18, parent or guardian must sign)

This offer, limited to one per household, expires June 30, 1985. Terms and prices subject to change. Your enrollment is subject to acceptance by Simon & Schuster Enterprises.

Silhouette Intimate Moments is a service mark and trademark of Simon & Schuster, Inc.

Silhouette Intimate Moments

Coming Next Month

A WOMAN WITHOUT LIES
by Elizabeth Lowell

•

DISTANT WORLDS
by Monica Barrie

•

SCOUNDREL
by Pamela Wallace

•

DEMON LOVER
by Kathleen Creighton